The L   Carmichael

SOFIE LAGUNA

illustrated by MARC MCBRIDE

ALLEN&UNWIN

SYDNEY·MELBOURNE·AUCKLAND·LONDON

First published by Allen & Unwin in 2021

Allen & Unwin
83 Alexander Street
Crows Nest NSW 2065
Australia
Phone: (61 2) 8425 0100
Email: info@allenandunwin.com
Web: www.allenandunwin.com

 A catalogue record for this book is available from the National Library of Australia

ISBN 978 1 76087 857 3

For teaching resources, explore
www.allenandunwin.com/resources/for-teachers

Illustration technique: hand-drawn with 2B pencil in Adobe Photoshop

Cover and text design by Sandra Nobes
Cover artwork by Marc Mcbride
Set in 12 pt Adobe Caslon by Sandra Nobes
Printed in July 2021 in Australia by McPherson's Printing Group

1 3 5 7 9 10 8 6 4 2

 The paper in this book is FSC® certified. FSC® promotes environmentally responsible, socially beneficial and economically viable management of the world's forests.

sofielaguna.com/index.php/books
www.marcmcbride.com

For Sonny and Milo

Chapter One

MATTHEW ZAJAC lay in his bed in his room at the top of the stairs. He was surrounded by library books: *Magnetic North, Into the Ice, Journey to the Farthest North,* and *Animals of the Arctic.* He opened *Animals of the Arctic* at a double-page spread of the Arctic wolf. The white wolf was cut in half by the crease between the pages. Matthew smoothed his hands down over the animal's golden eyes, its rough

fur. *The Arctic wolf lives in the boreal forests*, Matthew read. *As the frozen ground prevents the Arctic wolf from digging a den, it typically makes its home in a cave.*

He glanced up through the window above his bed, at the starless sky outside. The moon was full, and he could see rows of triangular rooftops belonging to the many other houses just like his. In the night skies of the Arctic, you could see the northern lights – clouds of pink and green and purple light that had come all the way from the sun, spiralling like the patterns on a shell. Matthew rolled onto his side and opened *Magnetic North*. When he read about the Arctic, he entered another world.

He turned to a picture of wide grassy plains at the foot of a range of snow-capped mountains. The picture was labelled *Arctic tundra in the summertime*. Matthew ran his fingers over the words. *Arctic winters are long and cold, while summers are short and cool. The average Arctic winter is minus thirty-four degrees.*

He lay back on his pillow. The northernmost point on the Earth was the North Pole – a place separate from the grassy plains, the mountains and the forests of the Arctic. The North Pole was a land made only of ice, which floated on the Arctic sea. Water that you could walk on! A land that never stopped moving!

Matthew put down his books and switched off his reading lamp. Downstairs, he could hear his parents talking about him.

It's because you let Matthew...You don't make him...

But I have tried to make him...If there was some way, don't you think I'd find it?

Their anxious voices rose and fell in waves. How many nights had he fallen asleep to the sound?

Matthew squeezed his eyes shut tight and saw the Arctic tundra filled with poppies and cotton grass and bearberries. He watched as the summer skies darkened and the snows began to fall, covering the trees of the boreal forests, the tall and jagged mountains.

When winter was at its coldest, minus forty degrees in the North Pole, he would sleep.

He was woken that night by tapping at the window. Matthew rubbed his eyes and sat up in his bed. *Tap*

tap tap. He wiped the foggy glass with his hand and saw a bird on the ledge outside. A black bird. A crow.

What was a bird doing here in the middle of the night? *Tap tap tap.* The bird was tapping at the glass with its beak. Did it want to come inside? Was it cold? Matthew opened the window.

'At last!' the bird said.

Matthew shook his head. Was he dreaming?

The bird said, 'I didn't think you were ever going to open the window.'

Matthew couldn't speak. What was happening?

'Matthew?'

'Wh, wh…' Was he really trying to talk to a bird?

'I am Lewis. Lewis Carmichael,' said the bird.

'L…Lewis?'

'We met today. You shared your cake with me. You remember me, don't you?'

Matthew did remember. The bird from the park. The bird with the broken wing.

Chapter Two

EARLIER THAT DAY, Matthew's mother had been waiting for him as he'd come down the stairs for breakfast, as usual. She'd been standing at the stove. 'Good morning,' she said. 'Hungry?'

'Need your strength, son. Growing boys need to eat,' his father said, buttering toast at the kitchen table.

'What would you like to do today, Matthew?' his mother asked.

Matthew had shrugged; had seen his mother glance at his father.

'Why don't you take your bike to the park and get some fresh air?' his father asked. 'There might be someone down there for you to play with. You know, kick the ball around?'

'Yes, Dad.'

'I'll pack some muffins,' his mother said, her smile hopeful.

Matthew had listened to the creak of his bicycle wheels as he'd pedalled down the road to the park. If only a sister would come along, or a brother, he thought, pushing down on the pedals. Someone else to give his parents what they wanted. His bike bumped unsteadily over a pothole and he frowned. Matthew wobbled when he rode too slowly. That would drive his father crazy. *Get some speed up, son! Come on, Matt! Straighten her up.*

When he came to the park, Matthew had leaned his bike against the bench, taken off his backpack, and sat. In the distance, he saw Mariel and Lee and Adam coming up from the slope that led to the river. They were in his class, and he often saw them together at school. He wondered what they did down there by the river. You weren't allowed; the school said it wasn't safe. His parents said it too. But Mariel and Lee and Adam were always going there. They seemed to be searching for things, and they were often muddy, climbing the rocks, the trees; looking up-close at things they found. Mariel carried a bucket. What went into it? Matthew wondered.

Taking his book from his pack, *Journey to the Farthest North*, Matthew turned to a picture of a sailing ship with a woman at the helm. She was wearing a heavy padded coat with a hood and was looking through binoculars, out to sea. Matthew read the words underneath the picture: *Dr Juliana Rossi travels to the North Pole*.

'Dr Juliana Rossi,' Matthew whispered.

He looked up and noticed Mariel watching him, and felt his face turn hot. Why was she looking? Lee too. What did they want?

Matthew returned to his book. *Dr Juliana Rossi has given us a new understanding of the Arctic with her magnificent pictures.* He turned the page and saw a flock of snow geese in migration. *Snow geese migrate in large numbers, for over three thousand miles, to warmer shores*, he read.

At that moment, Matthew glanced up and was surprised to see a black crow sitting on the back of the bench beside him, as if it too was looking at the pages of *Journey to the Farthest North*.

'Hello,' said Matthew.

The bird hopped from the back of the bench to the seat, and then onto the ground. As it pecked at the dirt Matthew noticed that one of its wings dragged, like it might be broken. He pulled the apple muffin his mother had made for him from his pack, tore it in half and tossed one half to the ground. The bird looked at him, its head angled quizzically, then came closer, pecking at the muffin.

Matthew looked up to the monkey bars, where a group of kids were swinging from the parallel ladder, climbing the knot ropes, somersaulting over the rails. He turned back to the picture of Dr Juliana Rossi, binoculars in hand, in *Journey to the Farthest North*. What was it in Matthew's body that stopped him swinging and somersaulting and climbing with

the others? Why could they do it, but not him? He glanced down at the black crow bobbing about the bench. It had eaten all of the muffin.

'More?' Matthew asked, under his breath.

The bird's eyes glinted.

Matthew had thrown the bird the second half of his apple muffin then stood up. 'I'd better be going,' he'd said.

As much as his parents wanted him to improve his physical skills, they grew worried if he was gone too long.

Chapter Three

NOW, MATTHEW FROWNED at the black bird from the park sitting on his window ledge. Though he remembered the bird, he would never have believed it could speak. Was he hearing things?

'I do remember, yes…but…'

'But what?'

'Birds can't talk.'

'Can't they?' said the bird. 'Well, I am a bird and I'm talking to you.'

'Yes…but…'

'Matthew, look up.' The bird hopped around, and lifted its beak to the sky. 'Up there.'

Matthew leaned out of his window. There in the sky was an enormous balloon – as big as a house, it seemed to Matthew. Its colours were glowing so brightly that it was as if the moon itself was caught inside the balloon. Orange, green, pink, yellow, blue, purple – great glowing vertical stripes. The balloon was attached to a large wicker basket, which was sitting on Matthew's roof.

'Am I dreaming?' he said aloud. Who was he asking? Was he asking the bird?

'No, of course not.' The bird gave him a short, sharp peck on the arm.

'Ouch!'

'You felt that?' said the bird.

'Yes…yes…' Matthew rubbed his arm.

'You wouldn't feel it in a dream, would you?'

Matthew didn't know. He was confused. What was happening?

'You showed me your book today, and I thought you might like to go on an adventure. The way your scientist did. Your Dr Juliana Rossi. *A Journey to the Farthest North.*'

'That's where you want to go?' Matthew asked.

'Don't you?'

'But it's impossible.'

'Why do you say that?'

'The North Pole is six thousand, nine hundred and twenty-two nautical miles from here.'

'Two days in the balloon, by my calculations,' said the bird.

Two days to fly by balloon to the North Pole? Not possible. Matthew leaned out the window. The cold hit his face, burning his nose and cheeks, cutting through the fabric of his pyjama top. The balloon swayed in the sky.

'Come on,' said the bird. 'We need some nautical miles underway before dawn.' The balloon tugged on its ropes and the wicker basket moved upwards across the roof.

Matthew rubbed his eyes.

'Matthew, my name is Lewis Carmichael, and I have found us a way to travel to the Arctic. Come on.' The bird sounded frustrated.

Matthew thought, If I am dreaming, what does it matter if I say yes to the bird?

'You want to see it, don't you? The North Pole? Reindeer? Polar bears? All that?'

'Yes...but...'

'But what, Matthew? Boreas is waiting!'

'Boreas?'

'The North Wind!'

Matthew thought of the boreal forests in his books, home of the Arctic wolf. Boreal – *northern*.

'Matthew! Let's go!'

The basket lifted a little way off the roof and

then landed again. It was slowly being dragged to the roof's edge.

'This is it, Matthew. Everything we need is on board. Hurry!'

Matthew took a deep breath, put one foot out the window, and pulled himself through. The tiles felt rough under his bare feet. He took a step and one of them wobbled.

If this was a dream it would be easy, wouldn't it? thought Matthew. But nothing was ever easy for him, it seemed, even in dreams.

'Matthew, we need to get across the roof before the balloon is pulled too far!'

'All right!' Matthew called back. As he took another step, the wind whipped at his hair and his eyes. He was very high up. At school, in the gym, he'd been the only one to refuse the climbing wall. When he'd tried to cross the swinging bridge, a teacher had to help him return to the starting platform.

'Keep moving, Matthew,' the bird said. Its wing dragged, almost touching the tiles, as it hopped unevenly along beside him towards the chimney. When Matthew looked down, he saw his street and the street lamps and the road. It was a long way to the ground. He turned to his window. Still open.

He could just go back, pull down the glass. Climb under his warm blankets.

The bird was ahead of him now, almost at the balloon. Matthew put out his arms and took another step. His heart was racing, and he was freezing. But he kept going, step after step, until at last he reached the basket. He grabbed its rim and felt it move forward as the balloon pulled on the ropes.

'Can you help me into the basket?' the bird asked him.

Matthew bent down and placed his hands carefully over the bird's back. As he lifted it into the basket, he was surprised to feel its body firm and alive underneath stiff, gleaming feathers. How strange it all was. A bird in his hands, a balloon on his roof. Yet things felt more real here, not less. He placed the bird onto the floor of the basket. At that moment, the balloon slid further across the roof.

'Quick, Matthew, climb in. Quick!'

Just as a huge gust of wind knocked the basket over the edge of the roof, Matthew toppled in, almost landing on top of the bird. They were off the roof.

Chapter Four

'NOW WHAT?' MATTHEW said to the bird. He felt dizzy as he looked over the side of the basket. He could see the park in the moonlight, the glistening river. Even though he was out in the cold night air, wearing only his pyjamas, it was warm inside the basket; he hadn't expected that.

'Now we need to fly her above the thermals!'

'The thermals? How do we do that?' Matthew

gripped the side of the basket as the balloon swayed.

The bird hopped across the floor. 'See here, the gas tank?' Matthew saw a cylindrical tank in the centre of the basket floor, beneath the opening to the balloon above. The tank was just like the one attached to the barbeque at home.

'I don't know what to do with that,' said Matthew, aghast.

'The balloon won't fly herself, Matthew! We need to release gas into the balloon, using the gas burner, to heat the air, to lift us to Boreas.'

'Boreas?'

'Yes! The North Wind, remember?'

'Oh…Boreas…yes.' Matthew crossed the basket to the gas cylinder. At the top was a lever, with *Open* written on one side and *Closed* on the other. In the air above it, attached to the gas cylinder by a shiny silver tube, was a metal ring – the gas burner. It looked similar to the ones on the stove in his kitchen.

Matthew was knocked to the basket floor as another burst of wind buffeted the balloon. Then he saw that not only was the balloon being hurled about, but it was sinking too – it would soon be on the street outside his house. Was that what he wanted?

'Quick, Matthew. Three seconds of the gas. No more, no less. Hurry!'

Matthew could hardly think. He felt sick as the basket swung through the air.

'Matthew, hurry!'

Matthew stepped up, took the lever in his hand, and turned it to the left as hard as he could. *Open*. A great hot noisy blast of gas shot into the balloon from the gas burner above him, which lit up like a giant pilot light. Matthew was thrown back by the heat. No wonder the basket was so warm, underneath a balloon full of heated air!

It was more than three seconds, Matthew was sure, before he leapt back up, a hand shielding his

face, and turned off the gas. The balloon continued to sink.

'We're still going down, Lewis!' he shouted. Any second now they would hit the concrete!

'It's all in the timing,' the bird called back. 'Just wait a little longer...'

Suddenly the balloon pulled upwards. Matthew

was again knocked, dazed, onto the basket floor beside the bird.

'Good work!' said Lewis Carmichael.

Matthew clambered to his feet, stunned. He had done it!

The bird hopped to the basket's edge. 'Matthew, take a look at this.'

Matthew saw that there was a dial connected to one of the four poles joining the basket to the balloon.

'You see, the needle will point to either *Falling* or *Rising*. Between the two is Boreas. We need to work towards keeping the needle pointed to Boreas as much of the time as possible,' said Lewis.

'The North Wind.'

'Yes. Boreas will take us all the way to the farthest north. The trick is staying with him. The balloon will inevitably rise too high, after you release the gas, then she will sink, and for a while we'll ride Boreas before we fall beneath him again.'

'Which is when I release the gas again.'

'Exactly,' said Lewis. 'You learn fast.'

Matthew wasn't sure that was true.

As the balloon rose in the sky, Matthew looked around the wicker basket. On one side sat a large wooden chest with *Supplies* printed across the lid.

'Open it,' said the bird.

Matthew pulled open the heavy wooden lid and took a blue coat with a padded silver lining from the chest. 'For me?'

'Of course, for you! Who else? But you won't need it until later.'

The bird was right: Matthew didn't need the coat. Being in the balloon's wicker basket was like being in a room with a fire burning – except the walls were invisible, so Matthew could see every light in the city.

'See what other supplies there are,' said the bird.

Matthew looked in the trunk. He found brown knee-length boots, lined with fur, and gloves made from the same padded, shiny material as the coat. There were boxes marked *Food* and *Water*. There was a small gas stove similar to the one he had seen at Cubs – Cubs had been his parents' idea – in the same box as dishes and cutlery, a frying pan and two tin pots, and a daypack a little like his own schoolbag. There was a second cylinder of gas, an enormous padded silver blanket, and a small leather case.

When Matthew opened the case, he found a pair of black binoculars inside, attached to a black leather strap. He pulled the strap over his head, put the binoculars to his eyes, and looked up to the sky. The stars were suddenly so close that he felt he might be able to reach out and hold one in his hand.

'Dr Juliana Rossi,' said the bird.

'Dr Matthew Zajac, don't you mean?' Matthew said, turning to the bird, the binoculars still over his eyes. He saw a close-up of a long black feather, a bright round eye.

'Ha! Yes, yes,' said the bird, hopping around on the floor of the basket. 'Yes. *Ha.*' And he clacked his beak: *clack clack clack.* 'Dr Matthew Zajac.' *Clack clack.*

'Do you want to see from up here?' Matthew asked.

'Oh, yes! Yes please.'

Matthew crouched down and put out his arm, and Lewis Carmichael hopped up onto his shoulder.

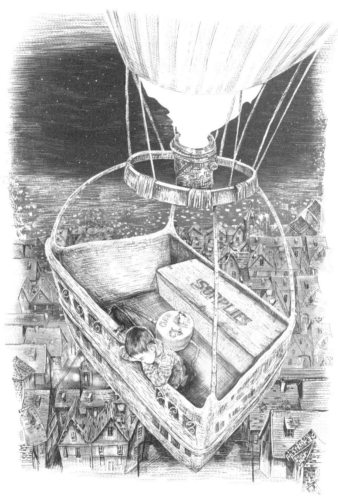

They stood together, looking out. Beneath them
were the lights of the town, cars on the road, houses,
buildings...and above them, the night sky; the sky
into which they were flying, higher and higher.

How endless and deep it was, with its shining moon, not caught inside the silken balloon after all, but up there, high above them.

'Beautiful, isn't it?' said Lewis.

'Very beautiful,' Matthew answered. He felt calm. Perhaps it was the way the balloon floated gently through the quiet sky, carrying Matthew and Lewis within its pocket of warmth. Perhaps it was the shining silver moon. 'How long will we be away?' he asked dreamily.

'We have enough provisions, including fuel, for three days in the Arctic. That includes seeing the forests and plains, and hopefully the North Pole itself, if we land close enough. But, Matthew, you understand time travels differently there, don't you?'

'I do,' Matthew answered. He knew that the North Pole was the only latitude without a time zone. There was no time there at all. *Because every longitudinal line begins from it, the North Pole has no time zone…*

'Time won't pass in the same way for us as it will for those at home,' said Lewis.

Those at home. Matthew didn't want to think about *those at home.* The noisy playground, the classroom, the teacher asking him questions. His parents talking about him downstairs, when they thought he was asleep.

…He has to get out and make an effort. If he just had the confidence…

If only he would try. Maybe more homework, extra tuition…

At school, everyone else was faster, as if the answers in class were just sitting there, right at the top, waiting. It wasn't like that for Matthew. He was too far away from the top. The answers flitted somewhere above him; it almost hurt to seek them.

A brother would help, he was sure. Or a sister. Matthew's parents didn't speak about having another child, but he was certain they'd been hoping for one.

And he hoped it for them. Someone who was more what they wanted.

Matthew pressed the binoculars to his eyes again and saw a hazy band of stars, one impossible to tell from another. The Milky Way. He lowered the binoculars. He belonged here – in a balloon heading for the Arctic. Matthew knew that the best place to see the stars was from the Arctic. Maybe he'd be lucky enough to see the northern lights – green and pink and purple, swirling there on the solar winds. He couldn't wait.

He rested his back against the basket and leaned out, tilting his face to the sky. There was the balloon high above them, the moon making it glow: moon-pink and moon-orange and moon-purple. They were flying over the sea now, every ripple outlined in silver. That didn't take long, thought Matthew.

'The balloon can move fast,' said Lewis. It was as if the bird could hear his thoughts. Matthew

liked having him there; liked the feeling of Lewis's claws through the fabric of his pyjamas. Hours could pass – Matthew didn't need for anything more to happen. He could drift across the silent sky, warm in the basket over the sea, the bird on his shoulder, forever.

'Time to check the dial!' said the bird.

'Oh…yes.' The dial. Matthew crossed the basket and looked at the disc behind the glass. The needle pointed to Boreas – they were riding the North Wind! He wondered why Lewis called it Boreas and not simply the North Wind.

'Boreas was the God of the North,' said Lewis. 'According to the ancient Greeks.'

'Oh. What did he do?'

'He was the god of winter. It was believed in ancient times that he brought the icy wind with his breath.'

'But at school we learned the energy that makes wind begins with the sun.'

'Yes. And icy wind comes when the sun heats the earth unevenly.'

'Isn't that science?' Matthew frowned.

'Perhaps Boreas is one way of describing that science.'

'Maybe both are true, then,' said Matthew. 'That the God of the North blows his icy breath, and that the sun heats the earth unevenly, to make him do it.'

'You are clever, Matthew.'

Clever? Matthew didn't know about that. He looked through the binoculars and saw a star shooting from one end of the sky to the other.

A great number of times during the night, Matthew released the gas into the throat of the balloon. He learned how far to stand from the heat. Learned to be prepared for it – the roar of the flame. Learned how to work the lever, how to use his hands. Came to anticipate the moment they would need more gas. *Well done, Matthew*, Lewis would say. *Good flying*. He would hop from Matthew's shoulder onto the rim of the basket and back again. *That's the way*.

When Matthew began to yawn, Lewis told him to sleep. 'Go on. Make a bed in the chest. There's plenty of room. I'll watch the dial and wake you when we need gas.'

'Are you sure?'

'Yes, I'm sure. Rest while you can.'

'What about you? Won't you need to sleep?'

'All I need to do is close my eyes, really. I can sleep anywhere. Anywhere I know I won't be eaten, that is.' Lewis clacked his beak. 'Go on, climb in. That blanket looks very inviting.'

'All right, then.' Matthew opened the chest, pushed aside the boxes and bottles, the second tank of gas, and climbed in. Lewis was right; there was plenty of room. And the insides of the box were made of padded leather, like the seats of a comfortable couch. Matthew snuggled into the blanket, soft beneath him, soft around him, and watched the stars.

Soon Matthew closed his eyes. He knew he could have asked Lewis how he came to fly the balloon onto the roof of his house. How Lewis had known. But he hadn't wanted to. If he asked, the dream might end. Matthew wasn't ready to face that. If Lewis had arrived to take him to the Arctic in a balloon, then so be it. He would go.

Chapter Five

'MATTHEW, WAKE UP...' It was the bird. 'It's the nautical dawn.'

Matthew opened his eyes. The rising sun had turned the world to gold – the ocean and the land and the sky, all gold. He climbed out of the chest.

'Isn't it magical?' said Lewis, from his shoulder.

Matthew blinked as he took it in: the sun rising from the line of the horizon, radiating its golden

warmth. He felt lucky to see something so…magical, yes, Lewis had chosen the right word. But the sun rose every day. It was there for him to see every morning, if he chose – ordinary.

'Breakfast,' said the bird.

'I'll check the dial first,' Matthew replied. The needle pointed to *Falling*, so he released three seconds of the gas, stepping back as the flame shot upwards.

'Well done, Matthew. I might have missed that. All I can think of is my stomach!'

Matthew felt quietly pleased as he opened one of the boxes of food from the chest. He found oats, a jar of honey, a pot of yoghurt, sunflower seeds and pine nuts, sultanas, pepitas and strawberries. In another bag he found cheese and ham, tuna and eggs, and butter and crackers. He pulled out the camp stove.

'We need gas for this,' he said to Lewis.

'Hmmm…but there's no gas attached. What do you think we should do?' the bird asked.

When Matthew's teacher asked him, *What do you think, Matthew?* he froze. Was that what was about to happen here with Lewis?

'Matthew, any ideas?' The bird hopped about the base of the chest. 'I'm starving, and I want something warm.'

Matthew closed his eyes and felt himself being rocked. The sea was beneath them, the sun above. He imagined himself travelling through a tunnel, twisting and turning, heading for a circle of light. 'We could see if there is a way to attach the stove to the main tank.'

'Oh...oh yes, yes, good idea. Why didn't I think of that?' the bird said, hopping closer to the tank.

Matthew took the stove over to the gas tank attached to the balloon and saw a small circular opening at the very bottom. He screwed the stove's loose pipe into the opening and pushed a red button on the little stove's base. The ring on the stove jumped with a blue-and-orange flame.

'Lift-off,' said Lewis.

Matthew could hardly believe it. He had done it. He had turned on the stove.

Matthew put oats and water into one of the tin pots and placed it onto the stove. At home, his mother made his breakfast; he never made it for himself. Oats, water. Wooden spoon. Matthew sat cross-legged on the basket's wooden floor and stirred the bubbling oats. A little spilled onto the stove and he glanced at Lewis, but the bird wasn't watching. Matthew kept going: stirring, watching the oats pop and spurt. Like lava, he thought to himself. I bet the God of the North would like this for his breakfast.

When it seemed ready, Matthew turned off the stove and spooned the porridge into two bowls. Then he added strawberries and honey. Honey dripped down the outside of the bowls. Lewis didn't mention it.

'Seeds for me,' said the bird.

'Coming up,' Matthew said, spreading sunflower seeds and pepitas over both bowls. The bird hopped down from his shoulder and pecked at his

breakfast. Matthew ate too. The porridge tasted creamy and sweet.

'What about tea?' Lewis asked, when he had finished his bowl.

'Tea?' Wasn't tea for adults?

'Yes, tea,' said Lewis. 'Who was it that said tea lifts the drinker to the realms of the gods? I drink it from takeaway cups in the park. Leftovers. You know, the last drops in the cup. But if I could have my own cup – what a treat…'

Matthew found tea leaves in the box. He boiled water in the second tin pot and added the leaves. Then he poured the dark brew into two cups and placed one of the cups before Lewis.

Matthew stood cradling his tea. His belly felt warm and full. There was the sun casting the ocean in gold. He looked up at the balloon – an enormous silent floating friend above them. What could be better than this? he thought.

'We need to wash the dishes,' said Lewis when his cup was empty.

'Oh…I suppose you're right, but how?'

'How? The same way dishes have been washed since the beginning of time. How do you think? A sponge. A little soap and warm water…'

Matthew heated more water in the pot, found a sponge and cleaned the dishes, the bird pecking at the fallen seeds, claws scratching at the wooden floor of the basket. When he was at home, Matthew helped his father dry the dishes; his parents wanted him to contribute. But this was different. There was nobody else to do the dishes except him. It was up to him.

The first day on board the balloon passed quickly: organising the supplies, preparing food, flying the craft. Matthew came to know, without needing to see the dial, when Boreas, God of the North, was carrying the balloon; when they had fallen beneath him; and when they were riding above. Matthew released the gas as it was needed, for three seconds each time, and the balloon flew on.

They were sitting on the supplies chest drinking tea when Lewis asked him, 'Why the Arctic, Matthew?'

Matthew shrugged.

'Matthew?'

'I don't know.'

'But you must have ideas about why.' Lewis pecked at the pepita seeds Matthew had scattered for him over the lid of the chest.

'No...I don't know.'

'Matthew, we have six thousand, nine hundred and twenty-two nautical miles to cover. Please, tell me, why the Arctic? Please try to find the words. If I, a humble crow, can find words, then you, a clever schoolboy, surely can. Why the Arctic? You know it's cold, right?' He dipped his beak into his tea. 'Seriously cold. And dangerous.' He broke a seed into two. 'Have you ever seen the tusk of a walrus? Those things grow to a hundred centimetres! And sharp!'

'I think…it's…there's a lot of…space…in the Arctic,' said Matthew. How pathetic his answer must sound.

But Lewis didn't seem to think it was a pathetic answer. 'Oh, yes, yes, that I can understand. The need for space.' He dipped his beak into his cup and drank. 'So little of it in town. Yes. Well, the Arctic will give us plenty of space. There's nobody at all in the North Pole. Uninhabitable, I hear. Except for the Arctic foxes. A crow's nightmare.'

'It's…the Arctic is…'

'Yes?'

'Wild.'

'Yes. Yes. I see.'

'It's…secret.'

'Oh really? How exciting.'

Exciting. Matthew liked that. The Arctic: full of space; secret and wild. All his words. And *exciting* – Lewis's word. He liked them all.

'Have you told anyone about it?' Lewis asked him.

'About what?'

'The Arctic. Have your shared your interest?'

Matthew shrugged again.

'Matthew?'

'No.'

'Why not?'

'I don't know.'

'Come on. You must know. Why?'

Finding words for things was difficult. There were so many to choose from. All the possibilities. It was easier to keep quiet. But Lewis Carmichael wasn't letting him do that. 'Matthew?'

'It's…it's not part of…of everything else. It's separate.'

'Oh, I see. I see, yes. Yours. Of course. How wonderful. The secret Arctic. Your very own.'

'Yes.'

'Only, now you are sharing it.'

Matthew frowned. 'Who with?'

Lewis clacked his beak. 'Who with? Who with? With me, Matthew! Your friend, Lewis Carmichael!'

Matthew laughed. 'Oh, yes!'

By lunchtime the sky was dark-grey, and it was growing colder. Matthew's nose felt icy when he stood at the basket's edge. If Lewis was on Matthew's shoulder at the time, the tips of his feathers would turn white with ice. The four poles attaching the basket to the balloon were all covered in ice too, and when he looked over the side, Matthew saw grassy plains and forests between more and more patches of snow – it was almost winter here. Still, the basket itself remained cosy beneath the balloon. It was as if a spell had been cast: the whole world outside of the basket was turning to ice, while Matthew and Lewis remained protected within invisible walls.

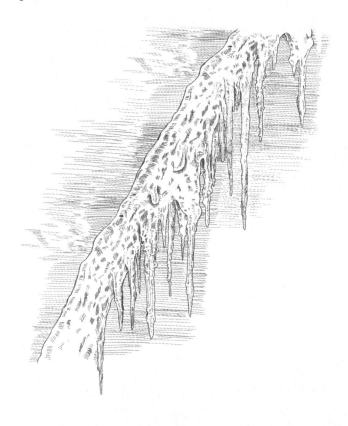

Chapter Six

LATE IN THE afternoon, Matthew saw shapes moving through the sky. He put the binoculars to his eyes and saw a great flock of birds, wings outstretched, flying towards them. 'Snow geese,' said Matthew, recognising the birds from his books.

Moments later, the white geese had encircled the balloon. Matthew felt the breeze from the beat of their wings across his face. They were flying so close he could have reached out and touched them.

'Put me on the edge of the basket, Matthew,' said Lewis.

Matthew turned to his friend. 'It's not safe, Lewis…'

'Put me on the edge, please.'

'But what if you fell?'

'I have taken care of myself a long time, Matthew. Please put me on the edge of the basket.' Lewis's tone had changed. It was serious. Cold. 'Longer than you have been alive.'

'But…'

'Matthew!'

Matthew did as the bird asked.

Lewis perched, quite still, on the edge of the basket, watching the geese. The flock circled the balloon for several minutes and then swept away, continuing in the opposite direction to the

balloon, spread across the sky in a giant V-formation.

Lewis remained on the rim of the basket, his feathers black against the pale sky, his back hunched. He didn't speak to Matthew, or encourage him, or peck at the floor looking for stray seeds. He didn't ask for more tea. He sat without moving, one wing extended, looking out.

'Lewis?'

'What?' Lewis kept his gaze on the sky.

'What happened to your wing?'

'Oh…that.'

'Yes, what happened?'

'Nothing much, really…'

'What?'

'I fell.'

'When?'

'Not long after I hatched. I fell trying to fly. The first time, actually. The only time.'

'Oh,' said Matthew.

'Yes, it happens.' Lewis half-lifted the extended

wing, so that Matthew could see a white quill at the base of each feather. 'I landed badly.'

Matthew thought about the myna birds that built their nests in the trees around his letterbox: the way the parent birds taught the babies to fly every spring. The young birds would land in the grass, stumbling, trying again, avoiding the cats and cars and foxes as best they could.

Lewis went on: 'At first I thought I wouldn't survive – my wing hurt me terribly. I was lying on my back in the gutter beside the path, and I thought if I allowed my eyes to close, I would never open them again. Then I saw, from the corner of my eye, a strawberry plant growing by the fence – and, peeking through its leaves, a strawberry. I thought, I want that strawberry. And so, somehow, I turned myself over, got myself out of the gutter and pecked the strawberry from its stem.' The bird looked up at Matthew. 'That was it. I had to survive.'

'And?'

'And what?'

'How did you survive?'

Lewis ruffled his feathers. 'My parents had given up by then; birds are harsh that way. I learned to be resourceful. To take shelter where I could. To hide. To find food. I stayed close to the world of people. I do better there. Not your untamed wilderness for me. Far too dangerous.'

Matthew nodded. 'I can imagine.'

'More crumbs in the human world, too. More cake. More food all round. Speaking of which, are there any more of those seeds for me in that chest?'

'Of course.' Matthew passed Lewis a handful of seeds. He liked to listen to the sharp crack as the crow pecked them in half. How clever and determined Lewis Carmichael was, to have been able to survive the way he had – how brave.

Matthew had the sense that they were moving faster and faster through the sky – flying in fast-motion, the way he'd imagined the seasons turning in the Arctic as he was falling asleep at home. When the clouds thinned enough, Matthew caught glimpses of sea, then land, then sea again.

That night, the winds became very rough. Lightning flashed, thunder rolled, and rain drenched the outsides of the basket.

'Lewis, are you all right?' Matthew called to his friend. By now the bird spent most of his time on Matthew's shoulder.

'Feathers!' the bird called back, as the balloon swung about. 'The best insulation there is!'

When Matthew needed to release the gas jet, the flame's fiery blast was reassuring. The wind roared, as if Boreas was furious. Matthew was glad they were not trying to fly against him.

As Matthew sailed the balloon, he forgot that he was in a dream; that it couldn't possibly be real;

that he would soon wake. He was too busy – and at times, too anxious. He had to check the dial and work the gas, and keep himself and Lewis fed. The bird demanded endless cups of tea. It seemed as if Matthew was always hooking up the stove, boiling the water. Minding it didn't slosh over the sides of the tin pot when Boreas blew.

Chapter Seven

WHAT A RELIEF it was to climb into the chest
and sleep. Matthew kept the lid open. 'You can
close it if you'd like,' Lewis said. 'I'll wake you.
I woke you from the other side of your window,
didn't I?'

But Matthew wanted the lid open; he was so
comfortable in the chest, and he wanted to see the
sky. He looked at the stars for a while, then slowly

closed his eyes. He imagined himself rocked, as if he was in a boat on the sea. What really is the difference, he asked himself, between the air and the sea?

He wondered if his parents were worried. When Matthew thought about his parents, from here in this balloon in the sky, it was as if they weren't real. When he thought about his home, he saw it in dark colours: far away and small and less important than this world here, in which he was flying the balloon with Lewis Carmichael. The balloon was real – look at it there above them, glowing and bright. Lewis on his shoulder, the balloon above, the nautical miles they had covered and the ones that lay ahead...these things were real. Every nerve in Matthew's body was alive, ready. This was real, and he was not alone. He had a friend.

Friends weren't easy for Matthew at school. He was baffled by the way other children knew how to fit in so well, how to belong. How to share what was important to them. He didn't understand what it was in him that made it difficult.

Friend. My friend, Lewis Carmichael. With the bird, it was easy.

On the second morning, at first light, when Matthew released the gas from the tank there was very little pressure. Not enough to make the usual blasting flame. 'Lewis, we seem to be running out of gas.'

'Out of gas?' Lewis hopped across the floor to the tank.

'It barely made any flame at all.'

'Did you open the valve all the way?'

'Of course – same as I've done every other time.'

'Then we must be about to land,' said Lewis.

'To land? Really?'

'Yes. The tank contained enough gas to carry us six thousand, nine hundred and twenty-two nautical

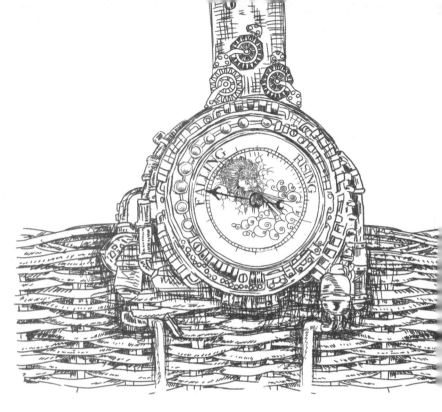

miles. Plus a little extra for cooking. And look at
the gauge – the balloon is falling.'

'So, what do we do now?'

'There is nothing for us to do but brace ourselves.'

Matthew gripped the edge of the basket, his
heart pounding. The balloon was still flying over
the ocean – the Arctic Ocean! – but an icy shore
was fast approaching. Further inland, in the distance,

he could see grasslands partially covered in ice and, beyond that, a range of snow-capped mountains encircled by forest. He recognised these as the Arctic tundra and the boreal forests. Beyond the shore, further out to sea, all he saw was white. Could that be the North Pole?

Matthew did not see houses or streets or buildings or towns out there. He did not see people. He felt as if he was the last person left in the world. Every part of him tingled. He had dreamed and read and thought about the Arctic and the North Pole for as long as he could remember. And he had done it secretly. It was a place that could not be touched by the demands and the ordinariness of the world in which he lived. And now he was here.

As they fell further and further below Boreas, Matthew saw snow on the sleeves of his pyjamas; he turned his face to the sky and felt snowflakes on his cheeks. And through the falling snow, always, was the balloon – a translucent bauble of bright silk against the sky. *Down, down, down.* The basket rocked and swung as they crossed the thermals. Matthew planted himself in a corner with Lewis on his shoulder and braced himself.

Chapter Eight

SLAM! THE BALLOON hit the ground, sending Matthew and the bird flying across the basket floor. Then it lifted a little way from the ground before slamming down again, skidding along the ice. Matthew and Lewis slid back across the basket, hitting the other side, the air forced from Matthew's lungs. They rose one last time – Matthew felt his

stomach turn – then dropped heavily, finally coming to a standstill. Matthew's chest heaved. 'Lewis, are you all right?'

Lewis peeked out from behind Matthew. 'Y… y…yes. I believe so. What about you?'

'I'm all right.' Matthew got to his feet, rubbing his back, his bruised knees and elbows. Snow fell softly onto his face, his pyjamas.

The balloon had landed close to the shore – the shore of the Arctic Ocean itself. How often he had looked at it on the pages of his books: covered in tracts of ice, the coldest ocean in the world, the least known, the most remote. Now he, Matthew Zajac, was seeing it for himself. And out there somewhere on this ocean was the North Magnetic Pole, floating on the ice.

Even though it was millions of years old, to Matthew the landscape appeared new. It was a country made new by ice. By snow and cold. He looked behind them at the tundra, partially covered in snow – and, in the distance, the forest and the mountains. In winter he knew that both tundra and mountains would be covered in snow and the sun wouldn't rise; that nothing could be seen at all.

'Let's take a walk to the shore, shall we?' Lewis said.

Matthew climbed over the rim of the basket. As soon as he was on the snow, the cold took his breath away.

'You'll need the coat,' said Lewis. 'Boots, too. And gloves. Don't forget the gloves.'

'Yes,' said Matthew, quickly climbing back into

the basket. He was already shivering from the seconds he'd spent outside the balloon's heat. He had never felt a cold like it. He opened the chest and put on the coat, the boots and the gloves. How well everything fit him – he was immediately warm. 'Why don't you hop into the hood?' he said to Lewis.

'Oh…wonderful…yes, why not?' The bird settled himself inside the hood, his head peeking out the side.

Matthew's boots crunched on the icy grass as he walked down to the shore, the binoculars dangling from their leather strap around his neck. His legs felt wobbly after so many hours on board the balloon. But it felt good to be walking again, with the air fresh and cold in his lungs.

When they reached the shore, Matthew had never seen so many birds at once. They were on the icy sand and over the water – diving, swooping, squabbling over fish. There were gannets and

ducks, bright-faced puffins, barnacle geese and
razorbills, Arctic terns, and snow geese like the
ones they had seen on the way here. Matthew
knew all the names from his books. Not like at
school, where he forgot the names for things he
was supposed to know.

'See the skua!' he said to Lewis. 'And there is the
little auk.'

'You have quite the memory, Matthew,' said Lewis.

When Matthew pressed the binoculars to his eyes, he saw king eiders out at sea – so many that the ocean seemed made of ducks. They bobbed and dipped their heads, their cheeks bright-yellow, and preened their sleek feathers. Is it always like this? he wondered. So many birds? Or are they putting on a show just for us?

He could sense the change in Lewis.

'Can you set me down, please?' the bird asked.

Matthew knew better than to argue. He placed his friend on the shore.

Lewis stood with the cold waves washing over his claws and watched the birds play and hunt and fly and dive. What a sound they made. How many there were, so full of life. Lewis – who seemed so sure of himself at other times – appeared out of place, perched on the sand with his head hunched between his wings.

'Come on.' Matthew crouched and held out his arm. Lewis hopped on, then up onto his shoulder. 'Let's get back to the balloon.'

'Yes, yes. You are right. Plans to make. All that.'

The balloon was still floating taut above the basket, bright against the snow. 'The balloon will remain just buoyant enough for us to fill it with the second tank of gas the day we leave,' Lewis said when they returned to the basket.

'Oh, I see,' Matthew answered. 'Good.' But he didn't want to see. He didn't want to think about anything but this moment – certainly not about leaving. He looked out over the snowy mountain range. The sky was changing colour, filled with streaks of blue and white and grey. It was all so enormous, and he had thought about it for such a long time that he hardly knew where to start. What happened next?

'Breakfast!' the bird announced. Matthew appreciated the way Lewis could move from sadness to happiness. As if the feelings didn't mind each other; as if they might be friends.

'But after breakfast?' Matthew asked.

'How about we walk up the mountain and get our bearings?' said Lewis, running his beak through his feathers.

Matthew looked out again over the range rising up and down in a jagged wave, each tip capped in snow. 'But…which mountain?'

The bird answered, 'The best view is always from the highest point.'

Doesn't anything scare you? Matthew thought. Even though Lewis couldn't fly, even though he was unlike the other birds here, he wanted to try things. Hard things.

Matthew grilled toast over the stove's flame, and heated seeds in the pan. If he didn't think ahead – watched only the toast, saw only the seeds in the pan – he could do these things. He could grill the toast until it was brown and crunchy, and spread it with butter and jam, just as his father did at home.

'You're getting good at this,' said Lewis, clacking his beak.

'I am!' said Matthew, biting into his toast. How crunchy it was, both salty and sweet. Toast tasted better in the Arctic. Matthew wiped jam from his mouth.

'We'd better prepare,' said the bird. 'We'll need food for the day.'

Matthew packed biscuits, chocolate and dried fruit, seeds and cheese, and peanut butter and crackers into the daypack. Then he boiled a flask of water for tea. 'We can sleep here in the basket,' he said to Lewis. 'We only need supplies for a day, then we can return to the basket at night.'

'Yes, yes, good idea, up here for thinking, up here for thinking.'

Lewis hopped from claw to claw, clacking his beak, making jokes. His excitement was infectious; Matthew could hardly wait for them to be on their way.

Chapter Nine

MATTHEW ENJOYED THE feeling of the pack against his back as he walked. When he had hiked with his school, he hadn't liked carrying the weight at all – it had prickled, and the straps had dug into his skin – but here it felt different. The pack connected him to the balloon and its basket and their camp, as well as enabling him to leave it. The boots kept his feet snug and helped him maintain his grip in the snow. He liked the feeling of Lewis Carmichael on his shoulder, too – hearing his voice, the things the bird said, the little questions. Like: 'Beautiful isn't it?'

'Very beautiful.'

'Cold, though.'

'So cold.'

'Oh, yes, yes, cold as ice, ha ha.' *Clack clack.*

Matthew trudged across the snow, working hard not to slip and fall, breathing heavily – the cold

clean air, in and out. He kept his eyes on the highest mountain in the range ahead: its cap of snow, the snow-covered trees at its base. The sun was rising higher in the sky, white against grey. The bird on his shoulder began to sing.

In all the world, I never did see, I never did see.

In all the world, I never did see, I never did see.

Oh yes, oh yes, in all the world.

Then he stopped singing and encouraged Matthew. 'That's the way, good work, Matthew, keep it up, warmer all the time, aren't we?'

When they reached the mountain's timberline, the land began to steepen. Black, leafless tree branches were covered in so much snow they seemed about to break. Matthew remembered pictures of Dr Juliana Rossi, in *Journey to the Farthest North*, trekking across the ice with two long steel walking poles. Matthew stooped to pick up a fallen branch almost his height. The bumpy stick was a good fit in his gloved hand. He poked the stick into the icy ground and pulled himself forward.

'Ah, yes...a walking stick,' said Lewis. 'Well done.'

'It helps,' said Matthew.

'But it's not quite ready...' said Lewis from his shoulder. 'If you don't mind me saying.'

'What do you mean?' Matthew asked.

'Your stick.' Lewis turned his head and plucked a long black feather from his broken wing.

'Oh...Lewis!'

'Go on – see what you can do with it.'

Matthew took the feather from Lewis's beak and stuck its quill through a small crack at the top of his stick. There it was, his walking pole – a black feather sprouting from a bumpy branch.

'Perfect,' said Matthew.

'Perfect,' said Lewis.

Matthew used his walking pole to break the icy ground ahead. He liked the rhythm he made as he went along – *left foot right foot stick in the ice! Left foot right foot stick in the ice!* Lewis's feather at the top was like a tiny black sail, changing direction in the wind.

Matthew stopped a moment to look back down the mountain, the way they had come. He could see the balloon peeking between the trees, like a giant glowing landmark. Home base.

'Matthew...' Lewis whispered.

Matthew turned ahead and gasped. Coming down the mountain, between the trees, was a polar bear. He froze. How many nights had he lain in bed tracing the outline of a polar bear's thick white coat on the pages of his books? But this was real. Dangerous! The bear swung around, looking behind her. Coming slowly, clumsily, through the snow at the rear was a polar bear cub.

Matthew's mouth dropped open. The cub was pure-white, its eyes round and innocent. Matthew could see how young the animal was, how vulnerable. He kept completely still, knowing there was no animal more protective than a mother polar bear.

He was aware that he was shaking. That his heart was beating very, very hard.

The mother polar bear came to a halt.

'Oh dear…' Lewis whispered.

Matthew took in the bear's claws – long and sharp enough to tear him apart; her intimidating jaws; her thick fur. She could survive in temperatures as cold as minus eighty degrees. Nowhere was too cold for the polar bear.

The cub kept coming. Not towards its mother, but towards him! Matthew gripped his walking stick and bowed his head. He knew, from his reading, that he must not meet the eyes of the mother bear. *Early explorers learned to avoid the gaze of the polar bear.* The cub kept coming.

'Oh no, no, little one…off you go, go with your mother,' Lewis whispered.

Matthew could barely breathe. He didn't move a muscle. He could hear the mother bear snuffling and snorting.

Suddenly, she thundered across the snow. In that instant, Matthew looked up and met the eyes of the bear – dark and ferocious. A split second before she reached him, she swung towards her cub, barrelling into it with her great head. Roaring.

The cub squealed. The mother nosed it roughly away from Matthew, pushing it through the trees. Matthew watched as they left: from a distance, the mother turned once more and looked at him. Then she swung back around, and they were gone.

'Matthew, are you all right?' Even Lewis sounded jittery.

'I th…th…think so.'

'That was close.'

'Very close,' said Matthew, his heart finally beginning to slow down. It was the most frightening thing that had ever happened to him. He knew he had never been in more danger. So why did it feel like a gift?

'Are you able to keep going?' Lewis asked him.

'I think so.' Matthew felt light-headed. More light-headed than he had been on the climbing platform at school.

Lewis said, 'You're brave, Matthew.'

'I don't know about that,' Matthew answered. He didn't think he'd been called brave before. Or perhaps he had, but he hadn't believed it.

'I think you are.'

'All I did was stand there. What else was there to do?'

'I don't know. A lot of things. But you held your ground. Tell me when you need to rest, okay?'

'Not yet.'

'Hmm. Strong boy,' said the bird.

Matthew liked the sound of his breath coming hard, in and out, as they continued on their way; the feel of his footfalls up the icy trail, his walking stick in the ice. And he liked the bird's words. *Strong. Brave. You held your ground.* The words made him want to keep going. He hadn't known that words could be so powerful. Was it the words getting him up the mountain, or his own feet? Did the two know about each other?

Matthew looked around him. There was snow on the mountains up ahead and increasing patches of slushy snow underfoot. Icicles hung from the trees. The sky above them was now grey and white. Matthew had thought there was only one shade of white, but it seemed there were a thousand – as many shades of white as there were birds on the ocean. When he looked back through the trees, he again caught glimpses of the balloon floating between them: yellow, pink, orange and blue. Lewis sang.

In all the world, I never did see, I never did see, I never did see.

Of all the lands, of all the lands, this one, now, this one.

Of all the boys, of all the boys…

A little while later, Matthew rubbed his eyes. The branches ahead were moving – separating from the trunks of trees, splitting apart. Was the forest coming to life?

'Lewis, what is happening?'

'I...I...don't know.' Lewis sounded scared.

But then Matthew saw that they were not branches at all – not trees come to life. 'Reindeer!'

Matthew spun. They were surrounded: the forest was made all of reindeers. One called to the rest, a loud grunting call. Then the whole forest seemed to come apart around them as the herd of reindeer charged through the trees.

Matthew listened to the pounding of the reindeers' hooves, the snapping of branches, the shattering of ice as they galloped away. After that, the forest was quiet again. Matthew heard the sound of his own breath coming heavily in and out of his nostrils. The pounding hooves of the reindeer only seemed to remain now in his own chest.

'Whatever next?' said Lewis.

'Keep walking?' Matthew said, his voice shaky.

'Keep walking,' the bird answered.

Higher and higher up the mountain they went. Matthew felt alert – as if it wasn't only his eyes that were seeing, but all his senses. As if he too was an animal in the Arctic. Watching for danger. Surviving.

Eventually Lewis said, 'Shall we stop for a while? Have something to eat?'

'Yes,' said Matthew gratefully. He was used to seeing the classroom, his bedroom, the park…not mountains covered in snow, polar bears protecting their cubs, trees that turned into reindeer. He needed a rest.

Matthew leaned his stick against a large flat rock and brushed the snow from its surface. He took the flask of tea from the pack and poured a cup for Lewis. Then he unscrewed the jar of seeds, scattering some onto the rock. He noticed, again, the imbalance between Lewis's wings as the bird hopped about, pecking at the seeds and sipping from his tea. Yet Lewis doesn't seem bothered by it, he thought. As Matthew watched the bird – bouncing cheerily across the snow; clacking his beak and cracking his jokes – it was impossible to imagine him any other way.

Matthew drank from his cup and ate his honey biscuit and dried apricots. The tea was hot and sweet. The apricots were chewy and delicious. He took a deep breath of icy air.

'Hmmm. Perfect…hmmm…' clacked Lewis.

Matthew knew Lewis was commenting on the tea, but he thought that everything here seemed perfect. Even if it was dangerous.

'Ready to keep walking?' Lewis asked.

'Ready,' Matthew answered.

Lewis hopped back up inside his hood. Matthew appreciated the bird's warmth against his cheek. He pulled himself to his feet with his stick.

As they continued up the mountain, Matthew felt as if he was being watched. He looked up into the trees and saw a snowy owl sitting in the branches of a tall pine, observing them with yellow eyes.

'Look, Lewis!' Matthew whispered, pointing.

He knew that the snowy owl was an intrepid hunter, and the heaviest owl in the world. That it made its nest on the ground, and had to guard it from foxes and wolves.

'Oh Matthew, it's been following us since we entered the forest.'

'Really?'

'There is nothing a wild bird doesn't see. And a boy with a black crow on his shoulder is hard to miss.'

'Oh...' said Matthew, marvelling at the way the owl could keep itself hidden and see so much.

At that moment the owl swooped past Matthew and Lewis and disappeared into the forest.

They went on. It was very quiet – both of them, the boy and the bird, were in their own worlds, their own thoughts. Matthew had stopped asking himself some time ago if this was a dream; stopped wondering when and how it would end. He had too much work to do getting them both up the mountain as the trail steepened, became rockier. Sometimes he had to pull himself up by the branches that crossed their path. His legs ached, his muscles burned, and he found himself slipping more often. He was grateful for his walking stick, his padded coat, his sturdy boots.

'Up you get, that's the way. Keep going, not much further now,' said Lewis.

In all the world, oh in all the world.

Just a boy, one boy, in all the world...

The bird sang, and then he made a *clack clack clack* with his beak. Like a chorus – *clack clack clack*, close to Matthew's ear.

Finally they reached a wall of rock jutting abruptly from the snow, about three metres high. Above the rock was the snowy peak.

'What shall we do?' Matthew asked.

'Climb?' said the bird.

'It looks too steep...'

'Does it?'

Matthew felt suddenly annoyed with his friend. How quickly feelings could change!

Matthew breathed out slowly as he faced the almost sheer rock cliff. Then he fastened his walking stick into his daypack, checked Lewis was still secure in his hood, and began – placing his hands, and then his feet, into the small ledges in the rock, the nooks and the crannies. He felt himself stretched over the face of the rock like a spider.

'Oh, yes, yes, Matthew, we are on our way. Soon we will be at the top. Soon we will be there,' Lewis said from inside the hood.

Matthew moved carefully, finding new places to put his hands, his feet, not thinking, just doing. When he did look down, he felt sick, thought he would fall. But he kept going, using every part of his body.

The bird sang as Matthew climbed.

In all the world, I never did see, never did see.
In all the world, in all the lands.
One boy, this one boy.

Matthew's foot slipped. He gasped.

In all the world, oh I never did see, I never did see.
In all the lands, one boy, one boy…

His foot found another small hold in the rockface. His hand found a new nook to reach for. One last heave…and they were over the top.

On the snowy peak, Matthew pulled his feathered stick from his daypack and stuck it into the snow. He took a deep breath and stared out at the world spread before him.

Every picture in his books had been limited by the size of the page, contained within frames. Here, there was no frame. Here, the picture didn't end. Beyond those icy plains, the sea; and beyond the sea, a land that floated on the ice, drifting northwards. Matthew put the binoculars to his eyes and saw valleys and cliffs and rivers all made of snow. Everywhere was white.

Lewis shifted his position on Matthew's shoulder. 'If we get back to camp and head north along the shore, the sea itself can act as our compass…Can you see through your binoculars, Matthew, where the ocean turns to ice? That is where the North Pole begins.'

'I see! And it's not far from our camp.'

'About two hours' walk, I would say. Not far at all. We will walk there, perhaps tomorrow. I think two more days here will be plenty, don't you?'

'I suppose…' Matthew answered. Why did Lewis have to keep reminding him that their time here would come to an end?

'Matthew, look up.'

Matthew looked up and saw a white-tailed eagle circling the sky, its enormous wings outstretched. Immediately, all else was forgotten. He knew that the white-tailed eagle had the largest wingspan of any bird. As he watched it fly, Matthew felt as if a part of himself was up there in the sky with the bird, soaring above the mountains, flying over the ocean, searching for the shadows of fish. When he tore his gaze away long enough to look through the

binoculars, he saw the eagle's nest in a forked branch of a snow-laden tree growing between the rocks on a neighbouring mountaintop. He had seen pictures of an eagle's nest in *Animals of the Arctic*. The nests were built to last, with the eagles returning year after year.

Matthew and Lewis sat on a flat rock swept clear of snow and shared tea and peanut-butter crackers and chocolate. As he ate, Matthew put the binoculars to his eyes again and saw cracks in the bark of the pines, ice in crystals and, high in the sky, the eagle, circling.

'Mind you don't get peanut butter on the lenses,' Lewis said.

Matthew lowered the binoculars. 'It's even better here than I dreamed it would be.'

'Yes, because it's real,' said Lewis, eating the last of his cracker. 'But it's best if we head back now. We need to prepare the camp for the night. It will get much colder; we can't take risks in the wilderness.'

'All right.' But a part of Matthew didn't want to leave the summit. What would it be like to watch the sun set from here? To keep his eyes on the world below the mountain until dawn?

'You know it will soon be dark in the North Pole both day and night, don't you?' Lewis said.

'Polar darkness,' said Matthew. He had read a great deal about this: it happened when the centre of the sun fell below the horizon. No sunlight at all for eleven weeks.

'I am glad we're leaving before polar darkness.'

But Matthew wasn't so sure.

Chapter Ten

MATTHEW TRUDGED AND slipped and stumbled his way down the mountain – first over the rocks, then through the trees, and onto the plains of the tundra. Every part of his body was at work; he was sweating under his coat, breathing hard, and again was grateful for the support of his stick. Lewis remained inside his hood, sometimes singing and speaking words of encouragement, other times resting.

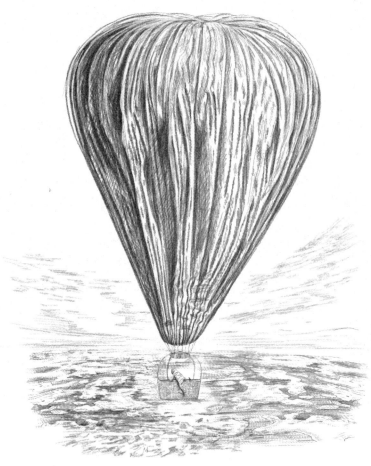

At last they reached the balloon: a rainbow floating in the snow.

'She has been waiting for us,' said Lewis. 'Though
she is not as round as she was. Still, there's plenty
of time until she has to be refilled.'

But Matthew didn't want to think about their next flight. He leaned his stick against the basket and climbed over its wicker rim. He was glad, after all, to be home.

Matthew took flour, eggs, milk and butter from one of the boxes of food in the supplies chest and mixed everything together.

'What are you making?' Lewis asked him.

'A pancake!' Matthew answered, pouring the mixture into the pan over the gas flame. 'To share.' He scattered sliced apple over the top. Drizzled some honey.

'Oh, lovely.' Lewis sat on the rim of the basket, running his beak through his black feathers until they gleamed, watching. He sang:

Never did I see, oh never did I see.

In all the world, a land, a land.

A boy, a boy…

'Dinner is served,' Matthew said.

Matthew divided the pancake in two, and he

and Lewis perched on the wooden floor of the basket, beneath the warmth still contained in the balloon, and ate. Matthew was hungry. He had never been so hungry! Today he had walked all the way up a mountain! He could feel that his body was tired – but he felt stronger.

The pancake tasted delicious. Crispy and buttery. Sweet with hot apple. Lewis enjoyed it too, pecking away, his beak clicking against his plate.

After dinner, they walked to the shore to rinse their dishes. There were so many birds – bobbing about in the water, or flying above it, hunting for food. Again, Matthew could feel the change in Lewis. He didn't talk or sing, or clack his beak. He just went still, watching.

'Let's get these dishes done,' Matthew said, swishing sand over the plates.

Lewis didn't move. He said, 'I would never survive out here the way these birds can. I wouldn't last a minute.'

'Well, neither would I.'

'Oh, you could do all the human things. You could live somewhere. There are scientists who do that, like the one who wrote your book – Juliana Rossi, was it? Humans can survive almost anywhere. But me…'

Matthew and Lewis watched as a flock of squawking gulls broke into a fight over the water.

'Come on, Lewis, let's get back to camp.'

Matthew crouched so that Lewis could hop up onto his arm. Lewis didn't move.

'Lewis?'

He didn't respond.

'Lewis?' Matthew said again.

'Oh, yes,' said the bird, as if he had only just remembered Matthew was there at all. 'Yes, camp...'

That night, Matthew very much wanted to stay awake in case they saw the northern lights, but he was having trouble keeping his eyes open.

'Why don't we get a good sleep tonight, and look for the lights tomorrow night instead?' Lewis said. 'There is still plenty of time.'

'Good idea.' Matthew was relieved.

He removed the gas tank and the stove from the

chest, leaving them standing neatly by the side of the basket, to allow himself a bit more space. After stacking everything else in the chest so it was out of his way, Matthew shook out the blanket and arranged it to make a sleeping bag. At home he didn't make his own bed, but when he came back from school there it was, made. He'd never thought about who made it. It must have been his parents, of course.

Matthew rolled up his coat so that it could act as a pillow, making sure to keep the hood out and open. 'Ready for bed, Lewis?'

'Oh, yes!' the bird answered, as if sleep was the best adventure of all.

Matthew picked up Lewis and placed him in the hood, then he climbed in too, tucking himself under the silver blanket. How cushioned and cosy it was inside the chest.

'Are you all right, Lewis?' Matthew whispered into the darkness.

'Yes, yes, quite. Thank you. And you?'

'Me too.' Matthew smiled, closing his eyes.

Lewis clacked his beak gently as he settled himself. *Clack clack clack.* Right beside Matthew.

In the night, Matthew was woken by the sound of crying. It was a lonely cry, as if whoever or whatever made it needed help. Matthew knew the cry. Or at least he almost knew it, but the full knowing was not yet there, as if it lay under ice.

Chapter Eleven

THE NEXT TIME he woke, Matthew was being shaken. For a moment he thought the balloon was landing again, slamming against the ice as it had when they arrived.

'Matthew! Matthew! What is that?' Lewis was awake too.

'I don't know!'

The chest was being pushed. Hard. Matthew

heard snorting sounds, close to the wicker. What was it?

Then whatever animal was out there growled.

'A bear, Matthew. It's a polar bear!'

A polar bear was attacking the basket! Bears could smell food from a hundred miles away. They had been lucky to escape unharmed when they'd seen one the first time.

Wham! Matthew felt the chest slide across the floor. Again, the bear growled. Matthew heard glass breaking, dishes clattering. *Wham!*

'Matthew! Matthew! What are we going to do?'

This was it. They were going to be eaten. He couldn't think, couldn't feel.

'Matthew.' Lewis sounded terrified. 'Do something!'

It wasn't only him this time. It was the bird too. Matthew couldn't freeze. He pushed open the lid of the chest.

There was the bear, luminous under the night

sky. It stood on its hind legs and roared when it saw him. Matthew was shaking. He crouched down slowly and fumbled for whatever he could reach in the chest – the ham, the cheese, the tuna. Then he stood again, eyes averted from the bear, holding the bags of supplies high.

'Food!' he shouted. 'Food!'

He shook the bags, then hurled them as hard as he could away from the balloon.

The bear dropped to all fours, lumbering towards the food. Matthew pulled the lid of the chest back down over him and Lewis, who was trembling.

'L-Lewis, are you all right?'

'Yes, yes…I am all right. And you?'

'I am all right.'

'You did the right thing, throwing the food.'

'What if it returns?'

'It won't.'

'But what if it does?'

'It doesn't help to think of *what ifs*, Matthew.

You gave the bear everything that would interest her: the ham, the tuna, and the cheese.'

'That's true...'

'There is nothing else we can do. I don't think she'll return.'

'All right.'

After a little while, Lewis said, 'It was the same bear, you know.'

'The bear we saw today? The mother bear?'

'Yes. Though her cub wasn't with her. She must have followed our scent.'

'Really? How could you can tell?'

'I am an animal, Matthew. Don't forget that. I think she'll leave us alone now. She has her cub to take care of.'

Matthew hoped his friend was right.

Matthew slept in fits and starts, expecting the polar bear to return at any moment. In his dreams, he saw her bright black eyes, hungry, shining. He saw her thick white fur, her powerful body. But in these dreams, Matthew didn't feel afraid. He felt the strength of the bear in himself, her ferocity, her strength, her desire to protect her baby. He felt it all in himself.

In the morning when Matthew opened the lid of the wooden box, the first thing he saw was a gaping hole in the wicker basket.

'Oh dear,' said Lewis from Matthew's shoulder.

Matthew picked up the spare gas tank from where it lay on its side against the supplies chest. There was a dent in the steel. The bear must have thrown the tank in her search for something to eat.

'From now on we will have to keep everything in the chest at all times,' said Lewis.

Their dishes were smashed. Across the way, lying

on the icy grass, was the torn packaging that had held their food.

'At least the balloon herself hasn't been torn,' Lewis added. 'Though you can see how much she has deflated.'

Matthew could now see wrinkles in the balloon's fabric. Still, it was reassuring to see it there, a burst of colour against the white-and-grey sky.

'I think we need to lie low for the day,' said Lewis, examining the basket. 'Attend to the damage. We can walk to the North Pole tomorrow. We will need to be sparing with our rations, but so long as you can survive on a bird's diet, Matthew, we will be fine. How does that sound?'

'Sounds good.' Matthew nodded. They were only left with seeds, honey biscuits, nuts, a little of the chocolate, and some oats. But Matthew felt the way he had in his dream. He wasn't concerned about the hole in the basket, their depleted food supplies. He wasn't worried that the balloon was sinking. He hardly wanted to eat anyway – he was too excited. Yesterday, they had seen reindeer and eagles and been followed by a snowy owl. He had faced a polar bear – given her food. And tomorrow they would cross the ice! They would see the North Pole.

'What do you think we should do about this?' said Lewis. He was looking at the tear in the wicker basket. 'It won't be safe to fly until we mend it, but really, I can't think how...'

Matthew looked at the tear too, and remembered the polar bear's claws. How sharp they were.

'Matthew, any ideas?'

Why was the bird asking him?

'Matthew, we really can't explore until this is fixed. It's not safe. So, you need to think of something. I am going to drink tea.'

Lewis hopped over to his cup, one of the only dishes that hadn't been smashed, and looked at Matthew expectantly.

Why was the bird being so bossy? Matthew

wondered as he boiled the water in the tin pot. How irritating he was! After he had made the tea, Matthew looked again at the hole in the basket, trailing his fingertips over the jagged edges of the cane. It reminded him of the eagle's nest they had seen the day before. Made from sticks placed over and over each other. Woven together. Those nests lasted years…

'Lewis!' Matthew called out.

'What is it?' Lewis called back. He had abandoned his tea and had been hopping about on the snow gathering the torn bags that the bear had left behind.

'We're going for a walk.'

Lewis hopped back to Matthew. 'Where to?'

'To the timberline.'

'Oh…well…I suppose that's not too far. All right then. Yes. Important to stretch the legs…'

Matthew strapped the empty daypack over his shoulders and picked up his walking stick. Then he crouched so that Lewis could hop up his arm.

'Going to put some supplies into that backpack, Matthew?' Lewis asked, settling on his shoulder.

'No…not today,' said Matthew distractedly.

'Oh…oh, I see. Well, up to you, up to you.'

They walked across the tundra towards the mountain. Was Matthew imagining it, or was there more snow today on the plain that led to the trees?

'More snow every day, Matthew,' said Lewis. 'It's getting colder and colder. Polar darkness draws ever closer.'

How did the bird know his thoughts? Matthew wondered, breaking the ice with his stick.

As they walked on, Matthew heard the crying again. It was the sound of a baby, Matthew was sure. 'Can you hear that, Lewis?'

'What?'

'A baby. Crying.'

Lewis put his head to the side, listening. 'I can't hear anything, Matthew. It was a baby, you say?'

'Yes...I think so...'

'Well, it is a sound I know well. There are a lot of prams in the park. Babies crying. All that. No, I don't hear it.' Lewis shook out his feathers. 'Perhaps it was Boreas.'

'No, I don't think so...' But it didn't matter; Matthew couldn't hear the sound anymore either.

When they reached the timberline, which was easier for Matthew than it had been the day before, he went to a pine tree with low-growing branches. He brushed off the snow, then snapped away the twigs that grew from the branches and stuffed them into his pack.

'Oh yes, yes, I see, I see. Well done, well done,' Lewis said as Matthew dug at the snow around the base of the tree, finding more fallen sticks to put into the pack. While Matthew worked, the bird sang.

In all the world, in all the world.
Never did I see, never, never did I see.
In all the lands, in all the lands...
This one boy, this one boy.

Soon the pack was full, twigs poking from the flaps at the top.

When they returned to the camp, Lewis asked, 'Matthew, what do you plan to do next?'

'Lunch,' said Matthew, smiling.

'Ah!' Lewis clacked his beak. 'Lunch. Yes, that's thinking straight, ha!'

They ate their lunch ration of oats and seeds – Matthew was starving – and then Matthew said, 'Lewis, I need your help.'

'My help, Matthew?' said Lewis. 'Yes, yes, all right. Of course.'

Matthew tipped the sticks from the daypack onto the basket floor. 'Lewis, you've never had to make a nest, have you?'

'No, I can't say I have ever had the good fortune,' the bird replied.

'But you know how, right?'

'Of course I know how. I am a bird. But, Matthew, I am not planning on hatching any chicks here in the Arctic.' Lewis clacked his beak.

Matthew was already sorting the sticks into piles of similar sizes, close to the tear in the basket's side. 'Can you help me weave these together into the basket,' he asked Lewis, 'as if you are making a nest?'

'Oh, I see, I see! A nest...yes, clever boy!'

They worked together, weaving the sticks into the cane surrounding the gap in the basket. Matthew found that if he stayed right under the balloon it was warm enough to work without his gloves. Lewis

used his beak to push the smaller twigs into the cracks in the wicker, while Matthew worked with the larger sticks, bending them into place, entwining them and the cane.

Lewis sang as he weaved.

In all the world, in all the world.

I never did see, I never did see.

In all the lands, in all the lands.

Matthew was hardly aware that he had joined in – that they sang together as they worked.

In all the world, in all the world.

Never did I see, never did I see.

In all the lands, in all the lands…

They wove the sticks into the cane until Matthew's fingers ached. When they were done, Matthew sat back and surveyed their efforts. He was surprised: the place that had been damaged by the bear now appeared stronger than any other part of the basket. Unbreakable. As strong as the nest of the white-tailed eagle; as strong as the nest of an Australian crow.

'I think we must reward ourselves with tea,' said the bird.

'And chocolate,' said Matthew, grinning.

'Matthew! Matthew!' It was Lewis, in the night, waking Matthew through his dreams. It must be very late. 'Matthew, open the lid. It's the northern lights – they're here, they're here!'

Aurora borealis. Lights of the north. Matthew rubbed his eyes and pushed open the lid of the chest.

Wisps of light danced across the night, flaring and billowing. Matthew gasped as the light made shapes in the sky – geese and bears, and the eyes of owls and wolves – purple and pink and green. One creature moved into the next – birds became animals, animals turned into flakes of snow, snow dispersed into nothing but colour. Matthew was held spell-bound.

Finally, the lights danced away and the sky was dark again. Matthew was tingling, as if the northern lights had brushed against his skin. As if they were dancing inside him.

'You know,' said Lewis from the hood of Matthew's coat, 'in Norse mythology it was believed that the northern lights were a fire-bridge to the sky, built by the gods.'

'Really?' said Matthew, finally looking away from the sky. 'I read that the lights come when there is a storm on the sun. The particles of energy are carried here by the solar winds.'

'Yes, yes...how interesting. Well, a fire-bridge to the sky, storms in the sun. Perhaps both are true.'

Matthew nodded. Both were true. He thought to himself: This is where I belong. Where bridges are made of fire. Where the lights dance in the shapes of animals. Where the things I do make a difference.

Matthew settled back into the chest, pulling the blanket around him, and closed his eyes – squeezed them tight. Ignoring the insistent cry that came and went, he was soon fast asleep.

Chapter Twelve

THE NEXT MORNING Matthew put the jar of seeds into his daypack and was just about to prepare Lewis's tea when the bird stopped him. 'No need to boil the water, Matthew. I won't have tea today. We can't spare the gas; the balloon must stay afloat.'

'But you love your tea.'

'Let's just be on our way. It could be quite a walk,' Lewis said, sounding anxious. 'And we don't have much food. We can't waste time.'

The balloon had sunk further overnight, but Matthew barely noticed. Today they were going to walk to the North Pole!

'I hope we see an Arctic wolf,' Matthew said as he pushed the last packet of honey biscuits into the pack with the seeds.

'They don't travel alone, you know,' said Lewis. 'They live in packs – like all dogs, if dogs had their way. They are a real danger for a bird like me. Make sure you bring enough seeds.'

'But you know you'll be safe with me, don't you?' said Matthew. How different it felt – how surprisingly good – to be reassuring.

'Well, yes, I suppose. Yes. Arctic wolves are wary of humans, which means, by deduction, that I too will be safe. Hmm, still…' Lewis hopped onto Matthew's outstretched arm. '…I don't fancy meeting one. Now, let's walk, or we shall see nothing more than this sinking balloon.'

The ocean was a patchwork of ice and seawater. Walking along the shore, Matthew liked to hear the

ice break beneath his stick and his boots. He could hardly imagine walking without the stick now, its perky black feather cheering him on. He felt like a new person, a different person. There was no *before* here; it was as if he was only being made now, in this moment of placing his boots on the ice.

At first Matthew's legs felt tired from the work of the day before, but he soon warmed up. As they followed the shore north, he saw birds – terns and ducks and gulls, bobbing on the sea, flying up and swooping down.

'We're not alone, I see,' Lewis said, peeking out from the hood of Matthew's coat. It was the only thing he did say. He didn't sing, or speak words of encouragement, or chat. He kept quite still on Matthew's shoulder, watching the other birds.

After a long time, Matthew saw a large rocky outcrop ahead. He squinted against the light. What were those lumpy shapes covering the rocks? Were they moving? Matthew put the binoculars to his

eyes and saw a huge herd of walruses. There must have been a thousand, all in one place. They were enormous. The two tusks that jutted from their jaws were long and pointed. 'Let's go a little closer,' said Matthew.

'Yes, why not?' said Lewis. 'Yesterday you defeated a polar bear, so what's a thousand tusked walruses to us today?'

Matthew edged closer to the walruses as they snorted and rolled across the rocks, turning their great brown bellies to the sky. He watched, enchanted, as the animals slouched and clambered against each other, rubbed their whiskered snouts, their wrinkled skin, not seeming to care that he and Lewis were there. How could a creature as awkward as this on land swim so fast in the sea?

'I only wish I could snort like that,' said Lewis, clacking his beak.

Matthew laughed, and every walrus joined him, snorting and belching and blowing and whistling.

Matthew closed his eyes and felt himself part of a chorus – a thousand laughing walruses strong.

After the rocky outcrop there was more and more ice on the ocean, and fewer and fewer birds. Lewis seemed himself again, and Matthew was glad when he heard him sing.

In all the world, beneath all the skies.

All the skies, I never did see, never did see…

All was silent but for his friend's song. A light snow fell. The sky above was white and grey.

I never did see, in all the world.

In all the lands, just this one.

This one boy…

Matthew walked to the rhythm of the bird's singing. His feet, the walking stick, and the song of Lewis Carmichael – all in time. Up ahead, he could see that the ocean had turned completely to ice. He was dazzled.

'The North Pole…' he whispered.

'The one and only,' said Lewis.

'We're really here.'

Matthew knew the North Pole was not really a land at all; that it was ice floating on the sea. But knowing couldn't prepare him for seeing it there. It glittered, so white it hurt his eyes. What would it be like to live in a place so empty? Matthew wondered. A place so cold?

'Shall we head for that snowy shelf in the distance? Do you see it, Matthew, up ahead?'

Matthew used his binoculars and saw a small valley made of snow, leading up to the snowy shelf on the other side.

'We might get some sort of view from there,' said Lewis. 'It seems as good a spot as any.'

As they entered the North Pole, Matthew put the binoculars to his eyes again and saw clouds and snow, the shadows between them. He moved the binoculars from the sky to the snow, back and forth, sky and snow, and sky again, until it seemed there was no difference between them.

The next time Matthew looked through his binoculars, he saw a polar bear.

'Lewis!' he gasped.

But Lewis had already seen. 'Oh dear.'

Matthew adjusted the binocular lenses. The bear was standing over a cub. There was something in the way she held her body. 'I think it might be her...'

'Who?'

'The bear that took our food. The bear from the mountain. It's her, Lewis, I'm sure it's her.'

'Not again!'

'I think so.'

'Does she have her cub with her? I can't quite tell.'

'Yes, but...'

'But what?' Lewis asked.

Matthew could see blood on the snow beside the baby animal. The mother bear was nosing her cub, trying to raise it. Something was preventing it from moving. 'She is with the cub, but I think it's hurt.'

'Hurt? How do you know?' Lewis asked.

'It's just lying there.'

'Oh…We had better give them a wide berth,' said Lewis. 'The bear will be feeling threatened. Afraid for her cub.'

'Yes, you're right.' Matthew lowered the binoculars. He could still see the small patch of blood in the snow, even without them. 'But it's not right, just to leave the cub like that, is it?'

'Lewis, the mother bear…she would attack…'

Matthew remembered the first day he'd seen the cub – the way it had trundled down the mountain towards him, as if it trusted him. 'Lewis, can we just go a little closer and see if there is anything at all we can do?'

'I don't know if that is very sensible.'

'But the cub is in trouble.'

'Matthew, this is the Arctic. Every animal here is in trouble, every day, every minute.'

'I have to at least see if we can help,' said Matthew.

'It's very dangerous.'

'I can't just walk away.'

'Yes, yes, I can see that. Oh dear. Well, all right then.'

'You'll let me?'

'You are your own master, Matthew.'

'You can stay here,' said Matthew. 'Where it's safe. I can build up the snow around you, and you can wait for me.'

'Oh, for goodness sake, Matthew, I'm coming with you! Let's get on with this.'

Matthew wondered if anyone had ever had a friend as good as Lewis Carmichael.

Taking a very deep breath, he began to cross the ice towards the mother bear and her cub. The mother bear watched him. She growled as he came closer. Matthew felt his legs tremble and kept a tight grip on his walking stick. Closer and closer…

Matthew could see, now, that blood stained the

ice at the cub's paw. He could see that something long and pointed and white stuck from its leg. 'I think it's...'

'What?' Lewis whispered.

Matthew squinted. 'It looks like it might be...' He adjusted the lenses on the binoculars.

'What, Matthew? Tell me!' Lewis said.

'It's the tusk of a walrus, Lewis. It's speared the cub.'

'Oh dear.'

'The polar bear must have attacked...' Matthew said.

'...and the walrus fought back. Yes. It can happen.'

Maybe it was too late. The mother bear growled again, louder this time, standing protectively over her cub. Matthew stopped, heart hammering. What if she wouldn't allow him to get close enough to help?

'Please,' he whispered. 'I don't want to hurt your baby.' He ran his eyes over the mother bear's piercing claws, her massive jaw and teeth...What was he thinking? The bear shook her head.

'It's too dangerous, Matthew,' Lewis whispered. 'She doesn't trust us.'

Matthew knew Lewis was right – but there was the cub in the snow, and if he didn't help it, what would happen? How long would the mother bear wait before she gave up? 'We want to help you,' he said. 'Please...'

The bear stood on her hind legs and roared. Matthew held his ground. He should turn back, he knew – run. But he didn't move. Shaking, he kept his eyes lowered, away from the great pink mouth, the black gums, the teeth.

The bear dropped down, her front paws landing heavily. She walked towards Matthew. At that moment, Matthew looked up, directly into her eyes. The air bristled between them.

'Matthew...' the bird whispered. The polar bear growled.

Oh no, thought Matthew.

Then, to his surprise, the bear turned and lumbered away. She was leaving! Abandoning her cub! The enormous animal loped across the ice, then when she had gone a small distance, she stopped and faced them.

'Matthew,' said Lewis, 'she's giving us a chance!'

Matthew ran as fast as he could across the ice. The small bear lay on its side, whimpering. Matthew let his walking stick fall into the snow and crouched beside it, looking at where the tusk had pierced its leg.

'Poor little bear...'

He touched the blood on the ice, and the fingers of his gloves came away red and sticky.

'The wound is fresh,' said Lewis. 'That's a good thing. The cub won't have lost all its strength.'

'I need to pull out the tusk.'

'Yes. Yes...you do.'

Matthew put his hands on the tusk. The cub

whined, struggling to raise its head. Across the way, the mother bear paced back and forth over the snow.

'Quickly, Matthew,' Lewis said.

Matthew looked at the blood that seeped from around the base of the tusk. 'We need to have a bandage ready,' he said.

'A bandage?'

'Yes.' Matthew knew that if a wound was deep, it could bleed a lot. It had happened to him – he had fallen from his bike when he was first learning to ride, and his father had wrapped the cut on his ankle tight with a long fabric strip from the first-aid kit.

Matthew looked around him, as if there might be something in the landscape that he could use for a bandage. There was nothing but ice and snow. The cub moaned. The mother bear kept pacing.

There has to be something, Matthew thought. He looked down at his coat.

'Matthew…' Lewis said.

'There is nothing else.'

'But Matthew...'

Matthew was already doing his best to tear a strip from the bottom section of his coat. His gloved hands were clumsy. He pulled off the gloves, but it was freezing – he couldn't use his hands in such cold!

'Can you tear the coat for me, Lewis?'

'Oh, Matthew.'

'Please, Lewis...'

'Matthew, you need this coat.'

'Lewis, you have to!'

'I don't have to!' Lewis hopped from Matthew's shoulder. 'But all right! If it's what you want. All right!'

He began to peck at the coat's fabric, pecking and pecking at the shiny material that had kept Matthew warm in the coldest weather in the world.

'Hurry!' Matthew said.

'I am trying!' Lewis kept pecking until a small tear appeared in the fabric around the hem.

'I can take it from here,' said Matthew, grabbing the coat. The bird hopped back and Matthew pulled at the tear.

'Oh no!' said Lewis.

Matthew tore away more fabric than he'd meant to. Now there was a large piece of the coat missing at the bottom on one side. Inside was a thick white downy stuffing. It would make a good bandage for the cub.

Matthew passed the long blue strip to Lewis. 'You hold this ready, Lewis.'

Lewis held the strip in his beak.

Matthew bent down over the cub. The mother bear came closer. Lewis nodded, the fabric dangling from his beak. 'Go on,' said the bird. 'Do it.'

Matthew put both hands around the tusk. The cub squealed.

'Pull, Matthew.'

Matthew kept his hold steady and pulled. The tusk slipped out from the cub's paw. Matthew

dropped the tusk, shocked by the blood that oozed
from the wound.

The mother bear roared. She began crossing the
ice towards them.

Matthew, hands shaking, took the bandage from
Lewis's beak and wrapped it around the cub's paw,

round and round, as quickly as he could. The cub looked up at him, dazed.

'That's the way, Matthew,' said Lewis. 'That's the way, keep going, nice and firm, you've got it, good work.'

Matthew tied the two ends of the bandage together as firmly and neatly as he could, tucking the loose pieces back into the bandage. Lewis hopped up his arm, and Matthew stepped back from the cub.

Suddenly the bear was thundering towards them! Matthew's heart stopped. The cub cried out again and then, realising it was free, pulled itself to its feet. The mother bear came to a sudden halt, and then entwined herself around her cub. The cub nuzzled into her side, then began to feed, the blue bandage firm and bright around its paw.

The mother bear stood on the ice looking at Matthew. Then she dropped her head.

'She is thanking you,' whispered Lewis.

'She is?'

'Yes. As you deserve.'

Matthew looked at the bear and dropped his head. It is me who should be thankful, he thought.

After a long moment, bear and cub trotted briskly away.

'And now, dear Matthew,' said Lewis, 'it's time to return to camp.'

Matthew picked up his walking stick. 'Really?' he said. 'Already?'

'It's too late to go any further. Your coat is torn, and night falls early here. We need to return.'

'But Lewis, we've only just arrived,' Matthew grumbled.

'Matthew, I understood your need to help the cub. But I must insist that we leave this place. Now. This is the wilderness. We have been lucky so far, but luck runs out.'

Matthew sighed.

'Matthew?'

'Yes, yes.' Matthew took one last look at the endless expanse of ice that surrounded them – the North Pole, land of his dreams. He stuck his stick into the ice and turned reluctantly southwards. Perhaps they could come back tomorrow.

They walked in silence against the icy, blasting wind. Matthew began to shake; for the first time since he had left his home, he was cold. Lewis had been right, he needed his coat – and now his coat was damaged.

'You did a good job, Matthew,' Lewis said eventually.

'I couldn't have done it without you, Lewis,' said Matthew.

Lewis clacked his beak, his body warm beside Matthew's cheek. 'Are you all right?' he asked. 'You're shivering.'

'I'm fine,' said Matthew, teeth chattering.

Snow began to fall heavily as they passed the

outcrop of rocks where they had seen the walruses. The animals were gone. Things can change so quickly here, thought Matthew. The snow and wind burned his face, his eyes. Lewis had retreated deep inside the hood – but Matthew could still hear him singing, even over the roaring wind.

In all the world. So far away, so far away.

This one boy, one boy, this world, I never did see, never did see.

In all the world, one boy…

By the time they reached the camp, Matthew was exhausted. He could see immediately how much the balloon had deflated. It was being buffeted violently by the winds, as wrinkled and loose as the skin of a walrus.

'It's all right,' said Lewis. 'We have the second tank of gas. Tomorrow we will fill her up, and she will be just as she was when you first saw her – taut and ready for flight.'

'Oh…good, Lewis.' But Matthew was confused.

He wanted the balloon to look the way it had, but he wasn't sure that he was ready to fly home.

It wasn't nearly as cosy under the balloon as it had been. Matthew did his best to hide how cold he was. But Lewis knew.

'The blanket will keep you just as warm as the coat, Matthew,' he said. 'And tomorrow we return home.'

Matthew wrapped himself in the blanket and finally stopped shivering as they shared the last packet of honey biscuits, the last of the chocolate. Only the seeds and the nuts were left.

'I am sure it will be enough until we return,' said Lewis. 'Now we had better get some rest. We fly at dawn.'

Matthew climbed into the chest and pulled the blanket over himself. He made sure Lewis was tucked into the hood of the coat, and closed the lid. For a while they were quiet; the only sound was Lewis clacking his beak, very gently, the way he did as he settled himself to sleep.

'I'm not ready to go home,' said Matthew. His voice was jarring in the quiet of the chest.

'Matthew…'

'I'm not.' Matthew had barely thought of home since he'd left. Barely thought about his parents, school. He had erased the thoughts and the worry the way the snow erased the land – turned them white. To nothing. Home didn't matter. His life was only beginning now.

'Since your coat can't protect you, we have no choice,' Lewis said. 'We have to return.' Matthew could hear the weariness in his friend's voice.

'I haven't seen the Arctic wolf,' said Matthew, turning away from the bird. He knew he sounded spoilt. That he was being unfair. But he was tired and grumpy. And the wolf was his favourite.

Chapter Thirteen

IT WAS THE crying that woke him, louder than before. Why couldn't Lewis hear it? Matthew wished it would stop – it made him feel sad. He pushed open the lid of the chest, sat up and peered into the darkness. Only the faintest streaks of light showed over the horizon.

Matthew saw a shadow moving through the trees. Golden eyes. He gasped.

'What is it?' Lewis asked.

'Lewis, it's a wolf! An Arctic wolf!'

'You saw it?'

'Yes!'

'Quickly, put me on your shoulder.'

Matthew placed the bird on his shoulder. 'There!' He pointed across the snow to where he had seen the shadow. Pulling on his coat and tucking Lewis inside the hood, he clambered out of the chest. Then he picked up his stick and ran. He would see the Arctic wolf!

With every step Matthew took in pursuit of the animal, the crying grew louder. Sometimes he thought he saw the wolf's glowing eyes, blinking at him in the half darkness.

Lewis spoke to him as he ran. 'Are you all right, Matthew? Watch your step. Careful there. Slow down, it's still dark!'

They had reached a cluster of snow-covered rocks. Matthew could see it was the entrance to a cave. The crying was louder here than it had ever been. The wolf stopped, turned to face Matthew, its eyes the colour of amber, lined in black. Matthew gripped his stick, stunned by the wildness and ferocity of the Arctic wolf. The wolf lifted its upper lip in a low growl.

'I only want to see you,' Matthew whispered.

The wolf disappeared into the mouth of the cave.

'Well…there it was. You got what you wanted,' said Lewis. 'The Arctic wolf, here, in its natural habitat. Now let's go back to camp.'

'But, Lewis, can't you hear that?'

The sound of the crying grew even stronger. What was wrong with the bird, that he could not hear such a cry? It made Matthew tremble. It was so unhappy. Where did he know it from?

'How many times have I told you that I can't hear anything?' said Lewis.

'It's a baby, crying.'

'So you've said.'

Matthew listened. 'It's coming from the wolf's den!'

'A baby crying in the wolf's den?'

'I'm going to take you back to the camp, Lewis.' Matthew started walking back through the snow to the camp.

'Good.'

'Then I am coming back here.'

'What do you mean?'

'I won't make you come with me. But I think there is something – some*one* – trapped inside the cave.'

'Matthew! That is where the wolves live. It is their home. You can't go in there!'

'What if I hadn't helped the cub? I am not asking you to stay with me…'

'Matthew, you're not thinking clearly. You're cold and you're tired. We've barely eaten. You must not go in there. I can't help you if you go in there.'

'You don't have to help me!' Matthew was running now. He had to get Lewis back to their camp. He had to help the baby. It was more important than anything else. More important than his friend's feelings, or his own safety. Why couldn't Lewis understand?

'Matthew, think! There can't be a baby in there. There are wolves in the cave, and that is all. Wolves! It's their home, and you have to respect that. You mustn't interfere – it isn't safe!'

'I don't care if it isn't safe!' Matthew shouted. He had always been safe, never taking a single risk. Never climbing too high, running too fast, falling too far. A baby was trapped in that cave. 'If there's a baby in there, I will rescue it.'

'But there can't—'

'I will rescue it, bring it home and give it to my parents!' Matthew hadn't realised his intention until he spoke the words. Now it was the only thing that mattered. A baby would make everything better.

Matthew kept running, as fast as he could, stumbling over branches, slipping in the snow.

'Matthew, please.'

'I have to!'

At last, Matthew saw the balloon, barely visible in the grey pre-dawn, sinking further every second. He threw down his walking stick, rushed to the basket, and set Lewis down on its wooden floor.

'No, Matthew!' the bird cried out.

'Wait for me here, Lewis.'

'Matthew...'

But Matthew was on his way. Not even bothering to bring his stick. Running as fast as he could. A baby was trapped inside that cave! He raced back through the snow, barely feeling the cold, his hunger, his weakness, following his own fresh tracks.

A wolf stood at the entrance to the cave, prowling back and forth. Matthew stopped. There was the cry again, louder, more insistent. The wolf turned and disappeared into the cave. Matthew ran to the entrance, stood there, heart pounding, wishing suddenly that he had brought his stick with him.

The cry grew louder still. Desperate. He knew that sound, didn't he?

Matthew stepped inside the wolves' den. It was pitch black. 'Hey,' he called, 'I'm coming!' He walked forward, the musty smell of dogs filling his nostrils. 'I'm coming!' he called again.

The wolves began to growl. There was more than just one. And it was so cold. Every part of Matthew was shaking. The golden eyes of wolves flickered in the darkness. How many were there? He kept walking forward, step after step, deeper and deeper into the cave, hearing, underneath the sound of the growling wolves, the cry, the lost human cry. The wolves could threaten him, but they would not stop Matthew from rescuing that baby.

'I'm coming!' he shouted again. He inched on through the darkness. The raw wild smell of the wolves was overpowering. They began to howl, but they would not scare him away. He could do this –

bring his parents what they needed. He would make them happy. Nothing could stop him!

At that moment, a shaft of light filtering through a gap in the roof lit the back of the cave. All Matthew saw were wolves. 'Where are you?' he shouted. Only wolves, everywhere wolves. Yet still he heard crying. Matthew looked wildly around the cave. Where was the baby? 'I'm here to save you!' he cried out.

Wolves howled. Matthew put his hands to his ears, pressing against them. The cry grew ever louder. Yet he could see there was no baby. The cry was not coming from inside the cave. There was no baby here, Matthew knew. The cry came from inside him.

Suddenly a wolf lunged for Matthew, pulling at his coat. Another leapt at him, knocking him to the ground.

'Matthew!'

Was that Lewis calling his name?

'Matthew!'

Yes, it was Lewis!

Matthew was on the ground, golden eyes all about him, wolf on wolf on wolf. He shouted, 'No! No!' and tried to kick the wolves away. But they lunged again and again. He shouted. Kicked. Screamed. Then suddenly he saw a great white bear, glowing in the dim light. The bear roared – attacking, wolves scattering. Whining.

The bird was beside him.

'Lewis!'

'Matthew!'

Matthew picked Lewis up and half-ran, half-crawled towards the entrance of the cave. He made it outside, into the first light of dawn, and stopped, his chest heaving.

The mother bear ran from the den too. She saw him there and lowered her head. Matthew recognised the cub waiting in the snow, the bandage bright-blue on its leg. The mother bear went towards the cub, and the two of them loped away into the snow.

'Lewis, are you all right?' Matthew asked his friend.

Lewis did not answer.

'Lewis?' Matthew looked down and saw that Lewis was bleeding. 'Lewis! Lewis!' Lewis's eyes were closed. Matthew held the bird inside his coat and ran.

What had Matthew done to his friend? His friend, Lewis, who'd found a way back to the cave to rescue Matthew – the same as he'd found his way out of the gutter when he'd first tried to fly.

When Matthew reached the balloon, he could hardly breathe. His heart was beating so hard he thought it would burst. He climbed into the basket. Then, as gently as he could, he took Lewis from his coat. His friend was sticky with blood.

'Lewis?'

Lewis's eyes were still closed, his head limp. Matthew saw that the blood came from his chest. He had been bitten by a wolf. Or perhaps it had been the claws of the polar bear; all animals were dangerous when they fought.

'Lewis.' Matthew fought his tears. 'Lewis.'

Lewis opened his eyes, then closed them again. 'Matthew…'

'Please, Lewis, speak to me.'

When at last Lewis spoke, his voice was very soft. 'Matthew, please don't worry so much.'

'Lewis…I'm sorry.'

'You don't need to be.'

'It's my fault.'

'Perhaps it is mine. It was me who brought you here.'

'But if I hadn't run back…'

'No need to find blame, Matthew, don't you see? There is no one to blame.'

'Lewis, will you be all right?'

'Everything will be all right.'

'But Lewis…'

'Shhhhh.'

Matthew tore the hood from his coat and set it in the chest. Then he laid Lewis as carefully as he could inside the hood. He took the last of the seeds and the nuts, placed them in a dish beside the bird. 'Lewis, can you eat?'

Lewis didn't move or open his eyes.

'Lewis, you must eat…'

The bird didn't respond.

Matthew lifted his head and saw that the sun had risen higher in the sky. Soon the balloon would deflate too much to sail. He had to hurry. If he could get Lewis home then everything would be all right, just like Lewis had said it would be. Matthew could take him to the vet. The vet would mend his injury.

Matthew felt strange – cold and dizzy and weak. And the cry, it was still there, coming and going inside him. But he didn't care about it anymore. He only cared about his friend.

He would make the bird tea. Lewis loved tea. *Tea lifts the drinker to the realms of the gods.* He would make his friend a cup of tea, and then he would fill the balloon and they would go home.

As he boiled the water in the tin pot, he heard Lewis singing, softly.

In all the world, never did I see.

This one boy, in all the world…

He is better! thought Matthew, flooded with relief. My friend is better!

'Matthew?'

'Yes? Yes, Lewis?' Matthew left the stove and crouched beside the bird.

'You need to go home.'

'We both do.'

'Matthew, things change...'

'What do you mean?' Matthew said. He felt himself trembling.

'I mean that nothing stays the same.'

'I don't want things to change.' What did his friend mean?

'Yes, you do. You want so many things to change. Make some friends, Matthew.'

A wave of pain rolled over Matthew's chest. 'It's not that easy.'

'How do you know until you try?'

'I know.'

'You don't, Matthew. You don't know. It hasn't happened yet, so you can't know. Try.'

'But...'

'Let me rest...'

'Yes, all right. I will fetch your tea.' Matthew finished making tea for Lewis. 'Lewis?' He placed the steaming cup before his friend, just as he had done so many times since their journey had begun. 'Lewis?'

The bird didn't answer.

'Lewis, I have made tea. Are you all right?'

'Yes, Matthew. Only, I don't think I will be going back with you.'

'But...' Matthew felt tears stinging his eyes.

'Matthew, take me down to the shore.'

'Lewis, I'm sorry.'

'You don't need to be sorry. Not for anything.'

'But...' Matthew felt lost. 'You don't belong here.'

'And where do I belong, exactly?'

Matthew looked out at the sea, where the king eiders and the pink-footed geese dipped and flew. His friend's voice sounded so weak.

'It wasn't only you who wanted to come here, Matthew,' Lewis said softly. 'I wanted to see it as much as you did.'

'Oh.' Matthew hadn't really thought about what had made Lewis do this – come all this way. What Lewis wanted.

'Please, take me down to the shore, Matthew.'

'Now?'

'Yes, now.'

Matthew tore off his gloves and held his friend in his hands. How fragile the bird's body felt.

He carried Lewis to the shore. There was, for the first time since they had come to the Arctic, gold in the sky over the sea. Out there, beyond the gold, was the North Pole. But Matthew wasn't interested

anymore. He never needed to see it again. He wanted only his friend.

'We're here, Lewis. We're on the shore.'

Lewis opened his eyes. 'Thank you, Matthew.' All over the sea were the birds – the terns and the barnacle geese and the gulls and the bright-faced puffins. Lewis lifted his head. 'You are a good friend, Matthew.'

'You are too, Lewis.' Matthew started to cry.

'Oh, Matthew…'

The birds came all about where Matthew stood – the terns and the plovers and the king eiders, and the geese that would soon migrate – and they flocked around him. So many birds that Matthew could not see through them. He was encircled in wings, as if all the world was made of feathers. And then the birds flew upwards, filling the sky, squawking and keening and singing and calling. When Matthew looked down, he saw that his hands were empty.

Chapter Fourteen

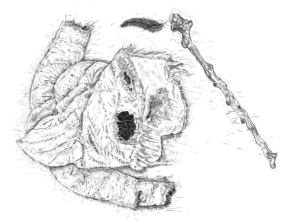

MATTHEW DIDN'T KNOW how he'd made it back to the balloon. He could barely see through his tears. Every part of him ached. He was so cold. Numb. He climbed into the wicker basket and picked up the second tank. It was lighter than he'd thought it would be. Much lighter. He looked closely at the tank and saw a crack at its base. When he opened the lever, he discovered that the tank was empty. It must have happened the night the bear had attacked the basket.

Matthew knew he couldn't return home without gas. But he was so tired, he hardly cared. His chest ached. He wanted only to close his eyes. *Just a small rest, Lewis, and then I will work out what I need to do.*

Matthew looked down at his coat – torn, red with Lewis's blood. He didn't want to wear it another minute. He pulled it off, tossing it onto the snow outside the basket, its frayed threads blue and silver against the snow. Beside the discarded coat was his walking stick – the long knobbly stick with its single black feather. Lewis's feather.

Matthew's chest hurt so much he could hardly bear it. He crawled into the empty chest, pulled the blanket over him, and closed the lid.

Matthew dreamed he was on the ocean with Lewis. He dreamed they were in a boat made of cane, same as the balloon's wicker basket, being rocked on the sea. He dreamed Lewis sat on the boat's edge, looking out.

In all the world, in all the world, never did I see, never did I see.

In all the lands, in all the lands.

Just one boy, one boy.

This boy. This boy.

And then Matthew was awake – properly awake. He sat up in the chest, pushed open the lid, and gasped.

Above him were the white bellies of a hundred snow geese, flying in a V-formation, each with a long thread of blue and silver in their beak. Every thread was attached to the wicker basket in which he flew. And there was his feathered walking stick, tied to the front of the basket like a figurehead. Matthew's heart skipped a beat: at the apex of the flock, leading the way, was a goose larger than the rest, with wings spread as wide as those of the white-tailed eagle.

Matthew looked over the side and saw the North Pole spread beneath them like a quilt of snow, its cliffs and peaks sparkling under starlight. The wild, inhospitable farthest north. It was beautiful, wondrous, precious – but Matthew did not want to stop there.

As the basket rocked and swayed, he lay back in the chest, keeping his eyes on the goose that was leading the way.

Matthew was jolted awake. They had landed. He unwrapped himself from the blanket and stood. The basket was on the roof of his house.

Climbing out onto the tiles, he saw the snow geese circling his roof. The stars and the moon behind him turned them as silver as the North Pole. As the flock turned away, the goose that had led them separated from the rest and circled, once more, over Matthew's house. Matthew watched, barely breathing, as the goose joined its flock, and was gone.

Matthew remembered when he had first made the journey from his window to the chimney, all that time ago. How frightened he had been; how scared of looking down. He crossed the tiles to his window now with ease, lifted it open, and climbed into his bedroom.

Immediately, he heard it. The crying. The crying he had heard from so far away. He knew now where it came from – where it had always come from. The light was on in the hallway. Matthew walked down the stairs and saw his mother at the kitchen table.

'Mum?'

She looked up, tears on her face. 'Matthew?'

'Son?' His father entered the kitchen. His eyes were red from crying. Matthew saw how pale his face was, how full of shadows.

'Hello, Mum. Dad.'

His mother looked at his father, then back at him. Then she went to him. She put her hands to his arms. 'Is it really you?'

Matthew felt heat come into him through her hands. 'Yes.'

She looked into his face. 'Are you all right?'

'Yes.'

His father went to him, took him into his arms. Matthew felt the warmth from his father go all about him. 'Matthew, where have you been?'

'I...I...' Matthew struggled to find the words. He didn't yet know what he wanted to say or tell. 'How long have I been...away?'

'Since this morning. You never came down for breakfast. You weren't in your room. Where have you been?'

'I have been to...to the North Pole. I wanted to bring you a baby.'

His mother frowned. 'Matthew, we don't want a baby.'

'You don't?'

'No, we don't. We want you,' said his father, tears catching in his throat.

'But…'

'Matthew,' his mother said, 'we love you.'

'We love you, Matthew.' His father squeezed his hand. 'I love you.'

'Please don't ever run away like that again.'

Run away? That was never what he had thought of himself as doing.

'We…We…It's because of us, the way we've been. I am sorry, Matthew,' said his father.

'I am sorry too,' said his mother.

Matthew could see how afraid they had been, of losing him. 'You don't need to be sorry,' he said into their embrace.

They held him close, and the crying stopped.

The next morning, when Matthew came down the stairs, his father was at the table and his mother stood at the stove.

'You must eat, Matthew,' she said, sounding

worried. 'You didn't have dinner last night. And I am sure you hardly ate in the North Pole.' She threw his father a look.

'I don't want you to do that anymore, Mum,' Matthew said.

'What?' his father frowned.

'I don't want you to worry about me so much. Either of you.'

'But Matthew,' said his mother, 'we love you. You are our son, and—'

'I know you love me, Mum. But I don't want you to worry so much. I need...' He faltered.

'What, son? What?' his father asked.

'I need you to...'

His mother's eyes filled with tears. Matthew didn't want her to cry. He really didn't. But he had to keep going.

'What is it, Matthew?' his father asked.

Matthew could see that his father was asking. Really asking. 'I need you to trust me,' he said.

'We do trust you,' said his father. 'That's why we

were so worried when you disappeared. You have always been a good boy. We know that.'

'I don't mean trusting me to be a good boy. I mean...trust me to...' Matthew worked hard to find the words. 'I need you to trust me to find my way.' He suddenly felt older than them. As old as the North Pole itself.

'Okay, Matthew.' His mother took his father's hand at the table.

'All right, son,' said his father.

Matthew hugged them. 'I love you,' he said.

Later that morning Matthew rode his bicycle along the road, the wheel creaking as it always had. He very much wanted to see the river that flowed at the far side of the park. He looked about at the trees and roads and houses as he pedalled. How warm and bright the sunshine was. How blue the sky.

SOFIE LAGUNA's many books for young people have been published in the US, the UK and in translation throughout Europe and Asia. She has been shortlisted for the Queensland Premier's Award, and twice been awarded Honour Book by the Children's Book Council of Australia (CBCA). She is also a highly acclaimed author for adults.

Sofie lives in Melbourne with her husband,

illustrator Marc McBride,

and their two young sons.

MARC McBRIDE is the illustrator of Emily Rodda's *New York Times* bestselling Deltora Quest series, which has sold over eighteen million copies worldwide and has become an anime TV show. He has illustrated more than two hundred book covers and ten picture books, including writing and illustrating *World of Monsters*. Marc has exhibited with the New York Society of Illustrators, been shortlisted for the CBCA Awards and Aurealis Awards, and has won the Aurealis Awards twice.